THE SPIDER:
SATAN'S MURDER MACHINES

MASTER OF MEN!
SPIDER ®

SATAN'S MURDER MACHINES

By Grant Stockbridge

POPULAR PUBLICATIONS • 2024

CHAPTER 1
THE MASKED MAN

THE MAN was a watchman, wearing the uniform of a private police agency, and he walked with his head bowed into the bitter winter wind that whimpered through Sutton Place. He moved swiftly, yet it was not the cold that he fled. Ever and again, he looked back the dark way he had come.

He was looking the wrong way, for half a block ahead of him, the shadows of a doorway concealed a curious figure. There was nothing furtive about the broad shoulders, superbly set off by the tailoring of a Chesterfield coat that covered evening dress; nor about the arrogant carriage of the head beneath the gleaming silk hat. He seemed a gentleman of leisure about to take a bedtime stroll, except for two things. The upper half of his face was hidden by a silk mask; and in his white-gloved hand there lay an automatic pistol, its snub nose brutal as a rattlesnake's head!

The eyes of the masked man were riveted on the approaching watchman, whom he intended to kidnap, but all his senses were preternaturally alert, as became a man who must fight both the police and the Underworld through every waking and sleeping hour... as became Richard Wentworth, who, in another life, was that lone wolf of justice known as the Spider!

None but Wentworth's ears would have caught the distant, slowly authoritative tread of feet coming from the opposite

This thing of steel could
be no living monster...

direction. Nor did he need to look that way to know that a policeman—a municipal cop—too, had entered Sutton Place. Beneath the black mask, Wentworth's lips drew bitterly thin. The officer's presence would make the Spider's task more difficult, but it could not swerve him from his purpose. More than personal safety was at stake. Four men had died this night, butchered with a brutality that had shocked to fury even the death-hardened Homicide Squad. And this watchman, whom the police had exonerated, held the key!

The watchman did not see Wentworth, did not hear him until he had passed the shadowed doorway that hid terror—then a thin voice reached out and froze him in his tracks!

"Hands down!" it whispered harshly. "Turn the corner left, and keep your head front, mug—*or you won't have no head!*"

On the lips of the masked man there was a slight smile. His friends along Fifth Avenue, in the exclusive clubs to which his name and wealth gained him easy access, would have been shocked to hear such accents from Richard Wentworth! The tones were crude, but the watchman recognized something else in that voice—and he obeyed! It was not an empty title that had been given the Spider, that of Master of Men!

The watchman moved stiffly toward the corner and, when he could no longer see the shadowed doorway even out of the tail of his eye, Wentworth stepped casually to the pavement. His movements were easy, his pace a careless stroll, although he covered ground with deceptive speed. The gun was ready in his fist. His eyes probed ahead to the approaching policeman!

At a distance of two blocks, the cop could see no details of the two men on Sutton Place. His back was to the wind and it pressed his heavy coat against his calves, sliced coldly about his wool-clad ankles. His eyes ached with the cold… That watchman was hurrying to his warm bed, off-duty, the lucky stiff! And a gentleman out for a bedtime stroll. Imagine a guy that didn't have to, going out in the cold on a night like this! The cop frowned a little then. Funny, both those guys turning toward the river where the wind was coldest; funny, both of them turning into a dead-end street! The cop shook his head, cursing the cold, and his eyes lingered on the dark entrance to the dead-end street. His pace quickened a little….

JUST TURNING that corner, Wentworth detected the quickened stride and swore softly under his breath. He needed no more than that quickened step to tell him the policeman was an old-timer, and already suspicious. That would make his deception more difficult—but he was still determined to take the watchman a prisoner. It did not matter whether the man would talk or not; it would become known that he was a prisoner. Wentworth intended to let the man's criminal pals know who was responsible so that they would come for him—and walk into the Spider's trap!

A long stride brought him close to the watchman, and he jammed the muzzle of the automatic against the man's ear.

"Don't try no funny business!" Wentworth said hoarsely. "This is a stick-up!"

His left hand ran deftly over the pockets of his prisoner, filched a gun and a few crumpled dollar bills. In that swift moment, his plan was fully formed. He would rob the man, knock him out—and then play good Samaritan for the benefit of the policeman, and the watchman! It should not be too difficult to start for a hospital, and finish up somewhere else where the watchman could be held prisoner! But he wished the wind were not so loud in the narrow canyon of the street. It rattled the skeletal boughs of stunted trees... and drowned out the footfalls of the cop!

"Listen, guy," Wentworth's prisoner whined. "Listen, you don't want to do this to me! It ain't healthy!"

Wentworth's eyes narrowed. It had been no part of his plan to question this man now, but if he would talk... and the policeman did not arrive too soon!

"Why not?" Wentworth demanded, and put a quaver in his voice. "I need the money more'n you! You gotta job!"

"I got friends!" the watchman said arrogantly. "You give me that money back, and—"

"What friends?" Wentworth snapped, hopefully.

The watchman made a sudden sideways lurch, started to whirl and grapple with Wentworth. It was the one thing that Wentworth could not permit. If the man glimpsed him, there would be no chance to kidnap him under the policeman's nose. Instead, Wentworth's arrest was certain... arrest and disgrace! Wentworth's blow was off-balance, but fiercely positive. It slammed under the man's ear and checked his turn. Before the man could recover, Wentworth struck again—and caught the watchman before he could slump to the pavement.

For an instant, Wentworth stood rigid, listening. He caught the tread of the policeman faintly. The cop was running toward the dead-end street! Wentworth swore raggedly, and his eyes flicked over the narrow *cul de sac* in which he stood. There was no place of concealment, no place to which he could flee, for the end, too, was sealed by a high wall. His eyes flicked toward the man whose unconscious body he held in his arms and Wentworth's eyes widened in amazement.

He had not known when he trailed this watchman just which private agency the man served, but the name was plain on the badge which gleamed on his chest: *The Drexler Protective Agency*. Wentworth shook his head incredulously. He knew the chief of the agency, Frank Drexler; knew him well. He was an honest and courageous ex-cop. It was incredible that Frank Drexler could be involved in such horror as had taken place this night, and… Wentworth jerked the thought from his brain. That would have to wait. Unless he could escape from this trap, which a running policeman was rapidly closing, the investigation of this horror would be impossible for Richard Wentworth. He would be locked up in a cell!

A grim smile touched Wentworth's lips. There was just a chance… Without further delay, he heaved the unconscious watchman of the Drexler agency to his shoulder and broke into a staggering run—straight toward the policeman who at this instant rounded the corner from Sutton Place!

"Help! Wentworth shouted as he ran. "Help! Police!" And he remembered then to slip the black mask from his eyes….

THE POLICEMAN jerked to a halt beneath the corner street light, and a finger of illumination glanced from a revolver in his right hand. It showed the bitter thrust of his cold-red-

7

dened jaw, the aggressive forward roll of his shoulders.

"Thank God!" Wentworth gasped, and staggered against the wall with his burden. "Get that man, officer! I think he killed this watchman!"

Wentworth sagged to his knees with the unconscious man, let him slump to the pavement. With his left hand, he ripped aside the watchman's loosened coat, gripped his shirt and tore it so that his fingers rested against the man's flesh. His voice sounded exhausted, and he felt the officer standing tautly over him. But Wentworth did not check his purpose. His left hand slid to a vest pocket and slipped out a cigarette lighter, thumbed open the base.

Wentworth twisted his face up toward the policeman, meeting the narrow suspicious glare of the eyes beneath the visor. "A man was lying in wait for this watchman!" Wentworth gasped. "A man in a long black cape, with a black hat low over his eyes. He looked like he was hunchbacked or something…."

"What?" the cop gasped. "Say that again… A hunch-back in a cape! Good God, man, do you mean… the Spider!"

Wentworth said, blankly, "Spider? He staggered to his feet. In the streetlight glare, his face seemed pale. Certainly, his eyes were stretched very wide. "God," he whispered. "Do you mean I was fighting… the Spider? I saw this man in the cape knock this watchman down, and stoop over him. He ripped open this man's shirt, and seemed to search him…."

Wentworth turned then, and stared down at his victim. The cop gasped hoarsely.

Suddenly, the beam of his flashlight reached out and laid its dazzling circle upon the watchman's exposed chest. That chest was curiously marked. On it had been tattooed a strange and awful design. It seemed to represent a gruesome face sketched upon a modern steel helmet… but it was not that which the policeman indicated with a shaking finger. He pointed to a figure etched in blood-red vermillion, a thing that seemed a living creature of hairy legs and poison fangs!

"Jeez, oh jeez!" he gasped. "You was right! *See… the seal of the Spider!*"

Wentworth's lips moved in a secret smile and his fingers touched absently the slim cigarette lighter in his pocket with which he had imprinted that seal. He had taken the only way to convince the policeman that there had been another man in the dead-end street… for the street ended in high walls. The cop would never have believed a third man could vanish from that trap; any man except the Spider! But that other design on the victim's chest proved that a Drexler man was involved.

"Listen," Wentworth said in nervous tones. "I want to get away from here. My car will be here in a moment… There it is now! Suppose I take this man to the hospital and call for help for you. You can stay here and stand guard!"

The cop was staring back up the length of the short dead-end street, toward the big limousine to which Wentworth had pointed. It rolled almost silently to a halt beside the curb. Its powerful motor made only a faint whispering beneath the long sleek hood. Wentworth gestured with a hidden hand to the man behind the wheel, indicating the unconscious body on the pavement. He needed to do no more than that, for the man behind the wheel was Jackson, his faithful comrade-at-arms who had fought through a hundred battles beside him. But even as Jackson stepped out of the car, the cop whipped about—and his revolver was pointed straight at Wentworth!

"Just a minute!" The cop's face was drawn and white "Just a minute, now. I don't like this. I don't like it at all. That car comes up too pat, and how do I know…" The cop swallowed noisily. "How do I know… *you ain't the Spider?*

NOTHING OF the tension that jerked all his nerves taut showed on Wentworth's face. But the cop could have no genuine suspicion, of course, and there was no proof unless… unless the cop searched him! He would find no proof that Wentworth was the Spider even then, but he would find the gun taken from the watchman, and he would find a silken mask! Easy enough, of course, to knock out the cop despite the leveled gun, but the policeman's trained memory would not be so easily overcome. The cop had seen his face!

Wentworth put exasperation into his voice. "Really! Of all the stupidity!" he said shortly. "No wonder there is need for such a man as the Spider! I've been warned that the police were even harder on witnesses than on criminals, and I was only trying to help a fellow human being!"

The cop had his shoulders against the wall and did not waver.

He was close to the watchman, who was lying strangely quiet. Wentworth had used his fists too often not to know the efficacy of each blow he struck, and he knew that the watchman should be conscious now; should have been several minutes ago. He  glanced covertly at the man's face and hid a smile as he saw that the eyes were too tightly closed. The man was shamming!

"You can say what you like, mister," the cop said doggedly, "but you ain't going nowhere until I can get the chief here!"

Wentworth shrugged slightly. "This is very easily settled," he said easily. "I saw this man here meet the Spider, and he's got the Spider's seal on his chest. They met on a dead-end street. It looks to me like this watchman is one of the Spider's assistants and they met by appointment, and had a disagreement over something. I'm entirely willing to go with you to headquarters. We will give that story out to the newspapers, and see what happens."

Wentworth's eyes were closely on the watchman's face while he spoke, and he saw the eyes open a fraction, saw fright begin to draw taut the lines about the man's mouth... If he could frighten the crook into striking the cop, and fleeing, it would be easy enough for Jackson to follow and take him prisoner. And the officer then would have no evidence and no complainant....

"If he's the Spider's man," Wentworth continued softly, "the Spider will come to free him. If he isn't the Spider's man, then he's a crook, for otherwise the Spider would not have attacked him. The newspaper story will make his crook pals think he's been two-timing them with the Spider… and they'll come after him, a different way! How does the plan strike you, officer?"

The cop shook his head, "Listen, I don't get what you're driving at, but if it's some plan to trap the Spider.…"

Wentworth saw determination clench the watchman's jaw, and behind him, Wentworth motioned Jackson not to interfere. Then the watchman flung himself into action! His foot struck upward hard against the cop's gun wrist. The revolver sailed high through the air and, the next instant, the watchman was on his feet and racing for the mouth of the dead-end street and Sutton Place!

The cop clutched his wrist in an agony of pain. "Catch him!" he gasped. "Catch that dirty louse and I'll crucify him!"

Wentworth turned casually to Jackson, "You might see what you can do," he murmured, and he winked deliberately!

Jackson needed no more than that for instructions. He snapped his hand up in salute, like the soldier he had been, and still was… though it was in the service of the Spider that he had enlisted now! As Jackson sprinted up the short street in pursuit of the fleeing watchman, Wentworth moved toward his car. The policeman was reaching for his revolver with his left hand, but Wentworth had no fears that he would be able to drop the fugitive. Jackson would overtake and capture him. This skirmish was won… and the story the policeman would give headquarters would help to notify the criminals behind these ghastly murders concerning the whereabouts of their vanished watchman! Meantime, Wentworth thought a call on Frank Drexler was indicated!

Wentworth reached in through the window of his car and flicked on the radio—and in the same instant, he heard a man scream!

WENTWORTH TWISTED about beside the car and stared toward the mouth of the street. The watchman had vanished around the corner into Sutton Place; he it must have been, who uttered that tearing scream.

As Wentworth stared, Jackson flung himself at the corner and then—Jackson seemed to go mad!

The whole scene was painfully clear in the bright pool of illumination beneath that corner street light. One instant, Jackson was hurling himself confidently forward in pursuit—the next, he was striving frantically to check his forward dash! He managed to grab the iron standard of the traffic light with his right hand, jerk to a standstill.

For that first, terrible instant, Wentworth thought that a bullet had found its billet in his comrade's body. Then he saw Jackson's head lift stiffly and stare down Sutton Place! His head was just beneath the green eye of the traffic light, and its ghastly glare fell across his drawn cheeks. Jackson's strong jaw was knotted, but there was no mistaking the rigidity that gripped his body. Jackson, who had dared death gladly a thousand times to serve his master; who had fought through a great war... *Jackson was afraid!*

Through that long instant, the tableau held, while the light still sprayed green across Jackson's face, while the scream of terror and despair sounded through the night. Then that scream broke, and Jackson wrenched himself free from the iron post. He began to claw for his gun. Jackson, whose draw was the swift strike of a snake, fumbled with a shaking hand for his gun! The traffic light changed to red, and the gun came free, began to spit its harsh thunder down the street. Beside Wentworth, the cop swore curiously and with his retrieved gun in his left hand, ran awkwardly along the dead-end. He had taken only three paces when a man whipped around the corner and charged into the street. The man ran wildly, with both arms flung high above his head, and the screams still came from his lips. It was the Drexler watchman.

"The Iron Man!" he shrieked. "God save me! *The Iron Man!*"

And abruptly, Jackson had abandoned his position beside the traffic light. He turned and ran swiftly toward Wentworth, and he was reloading his automatic. Twice he twisted his head about to stare back across his shoulder.

"What is it, Jackson?" Wentworth snapped.

He had his own gun in his hand and was striding to meet his comrade. The policeman already had passed him, was scrambling toward the corner. Wentworth knew the cold tightening of horror in his own heart, for he was remembering those looted homes and the distorted bodies of the four murdered men. They had been literally torn apart. And now Jackson fled, and a man screamed… *"The Iron Man!"*

Jackson whirled, and at the street's mouth, the policeman shouted hoarsely and unintelligibly… and then Wentworth saw—and he knew why the watchman had screamed, and why

Jackson had been stiff with fright; and how four living men had been torn apart!

The thing stood there for an instant beneath the swaying street light, a monster of steel, an iron man! Its head towered almost to that light, and the red glare from the traffic signal spilled like lucent blood across a gigantic torso. Arms swung from ponderous shoulders and the head—the head was a replica of the helmet tattooed upon the Drexler watchman's chest! Two blank eyes that were plates of glass glared emptily; the mouth had teeth like a steam-shovel—and the empty glare of those awful eyes was fixed upon Wentworth!

Even as the Spider ripped himself free from the paralysis which that sudden apparition had placed even upon the Master of Men, the giant in steel lifted a ponderous foot and set it upon the sidewalk. And under that colossal tread, the concrete crackled and broke like ice! A hand moved carelessly, and wrapped about the iron traffic signal standard… and that post snapped off with a sputter of electric sparks!

Once, twice, the robot whipped that heavy post about its head and then hurled it like a war-club at Wentworth's head!

CHAPTER 2
WHEN BULLETS FAIL

DEATH WAS very close to Richard Wentworth in that moment. There seemed a weight in limbs and brain, stupefaction over this thing his eyes saw, but his mind could not quite believe. It is certain that any other man would have been caught by that steel club and died miserably in his tracks. Wentworth managed somehow to wrench his frozen muscles into action. He shrank aside by a hair's breadth and the wind of the missile's passage whipped his silk hat from his head, fluttered the tails of his Chesterfield.

The policeman stood motionless, a paralyzed pigmy in the path of the steel monster. His gun was in his fist, his head wrenched back crazily to peer up at that travesty of a face. The watchman ducked behind Wentworth and crouched like a cowed dog and Jackson had his back flattened against the wall; automatic ready in his fist again.

"This way, officer!" Wentworth's voice cracked like a whip and, even in that paralysis of fear which gripped the man, the cop heard the accent of command and discipline stirred within him. He jerked up his revolver and fired at the monster. "Retreat, man!" Wentworth shouted. "Come to me!"

Wentworth whipped up his own automatic and took careful aim. He knew without further trial that the steel body would be impervious to bullets. Jackson's shrewd lead already had searched that out. One shot, Wentworth squeezed off. He knew that his lead flew true, caught the monster in one of its glass eyes—and nothing happened! The monster stood within a few yards of the policeman and slowly bent his head to stare down at the puny thing at its feet. A steel hand lifted casually....

With an oath, Wentworth leaped toward the Daimler. The policeman was fleeing in crazy, scrambling terror, and the monster was walking... slowly, ponderously. The tremor of that tread came through the pavement, seemed to vibrate in Wentworth's very bones.

"Keep away from it!" Wentworth shouted. "It can't move fast! Keep out of its way! Dodge!"

He flung himself behind the wheel of the Daimler, and wrenched it into gear, whipped it in a U-turn. The car was too long for that narrow street and he had to wrench it backward again while aching moments passed; while death moved with ponderous ease and on feet of steel. He glimpsed the giant, saw it lift a hand and point a finger like an accusation at the crouching watchman. The man's scream rose terribly, and then— fire spurted from that pointing finger! The scream cut off. The watchman was a twitching, dying huddle upon the ground!

Wentworth fought to hammer sane thoughts through his own brain. This thing of steel could be no living monster, of course. It must be a robot, though marvelously under control. A robot that could point a finger made into a gun barrel and kill with perfect aim! Wentworth jerked his head, struggling against the daze of incredulity that still gripped him. A robot was only a machine, an intricate and necessarily delicate machine. A profound blow, such an impact as would knock the thing to the ground, undoubtedly would disarrange its mechanism. It was simple, really. Whoever was master of this monster of steel had calculated on the terror its mere appearance would generate to prevent rational attack. He had not counted on meeting the Spider face-to-face!

Wentworth had whipped the heavy limousine about now, so that its nose was toward the robot. He swiftly flung it back-

· *RICHARD WENTWORTH* ·

ward until its rear bumper nudged the wall at the street's end. He would need all the momentum he could generate in this short dead-end street to upset that creature! He jerked loose the half-cushion beside him, and wedged it between his seat and the steering wheel, jerked the gear into second....

EVEN AS his foot hovered over the accelerator, the radio emitted a faint click... and suddenly a voice sounded in the car. That voice was disguised, but Wentworth recognized it at once.

He would always know that voice, in whatever circumstances he heard it, for it was that of Nita van Sloan, the woman he loved! He had been at an after-theatre party with Nita when word had come of the tragedy which had called the Spider to action—and he had sent Nita to keep watch on police headquarters while he flung himself into the battle! That was terribly necessary now since, on every hand, the police hounded the Spider. Her speech now could mean only one thing: the police were on his trail again!

Nita spoke softly, as if she would whisper those words into his ear, and her words would make no sense to others.

"The big blue cat," said Nita, "is going to the mouse's home to retrieve some stolen cheese!"

The words ran like an electric shock along Wentworth's nerves. *The big blue cat...* That meant Stanley Kirkpatrick, commissioner of police, who was at once Wentworth's friend and the Spider's enemy. And the mouse was Wentworth himself. *Stolen cheese...* Even as Wentworth jammed down the accelerator and drove the heavy Daimler toward the steel monster, the truth of that broadcast struck him, and shook him. It could mean

only one thing: Kirkpatrick was going to Wentworth's home on a tip-off that he would find some stolen goods there!

Nor did Wentworth even need to speculate on the nature of that loot, or whether he would find it! The loot would be there, and it would be loot from those three homes that had been rifled this night! By God, the enemy moved swiftly! Already, they had spotted Wentworth's interest in the case and moved to checkmate him—by planting in his home the evidence that he had been responsible for those lootings and awful murders! Strangely, Wentworth smiled. At least it proved human agency behind this robot!

Wentworth wrenched his mind to the battle at hand, but the delay had proved costly! The robot had closed up some of the precious distance Wentworth had gained, thus lessening the momentum which the car could build up. As Wentworth stared, and started the car leaping forward, the robot bent forward and plucked up the policeman from the earth! He grasped the screaming man by one ankle and, casually as a child might whirl a stick about its head, the robot spun the policeman! Two, three times he circled the helpless, doomed man… then flung the dangling thing that remained headlong toward the charging car!

A sickened horror surged through Wentworth. He tried to wrench the big car aside, but was too late. Headlong, against the bullet-proof glass of the windshield, the policeman hurtled, then slithered off to one side!

Wentworth's lips drew thin and bitter across his face and pallor crept into his cheeks. He leaned forward and flicked on the windshield wiper… shuddering involuntarily.

He needed to see very clearly to drive straight at this monster in steel who could perpetrate such horror. His anger seemed to lift the heavy car and hurl it forward, wringing the last ounce of power from the engine. His knuckles shone white as he gripped the wheel.

HE SAW the robot take a stride forward, and swing a foot like a football player about to kick off! And that foot was aimed at the radiator of the Daimler! In that horror-sodden instant, Wentworth knew that even this mighty attack would fail against the robot! On the moment, he batted open the door beside him and, as the Daimler surged toward the steel monster; he hurled himself toward the pavement!

Wentworth struck the pavement rolling in the same instant the robot crashed its foot against the radiator of the Daimler! He saw what happened then in flashing glimpses as he spun dizzily toward the curb and reeled to his feet. The thing was timed as beautifully as a drop-kick. The smashing impact of the robot's foot, whose tread could crack the concrete of the walks, caught the Daimler just at the front axle!

Fenders and headlights leaped from the limousine, and glass flew like a shattering grenade! The front of the car lifted, while the powerful drive of those rear wheels urged it on—and the whole machine spun dizzily aside, turned over and slammed against the wall of the house to the right! For an instant, the robot tottered. An outflung arm reached to the wall of the house, and the bricks crashed inward. A rubble of broken masonry clattered to the earth and plaster dust lifted around the monster of steel like battle-smoke. But it was only an instant, and then the

robot's head revolved slowly and the blankly awful eyes picked out Wentworth where he reeled, dazed from his heavy fall, against the opposite building wall. Jackson was beside him. His gun was spitting lead hysterically, but he might as well have been throwing pebbles at a seventy-ton tank.

Slowly, the right arm of the monster lifted... and Wentworth remembered that its forefinger could spurt lead and death! He flung himself sideways toward Jackson, carried the hysterically cursing man to the pavement... but there was no crash of a shot from the robot. Evidently the impact had partly disabled the monster! The thing was no longer braced against the wall but as it stepped toward where Wentworth fought to get Jackson to his feet, to retreat, he saw the left leg drag curiously. The Spider's charge had achieved something then! The monster was not working perfectly!

Wentworth reeled to his feet. There was no gun in his hand, for a gun would be useless. He stood slowly erect and watched the monster take another dragging step toward him... Then the robot stopped. The great head bent slowly and the blank emptiness of those eyes of glass peered down where the Spider stood, a pigmy in the path of Juggernaut. A moment passed, a long dragging moment while the two confronted each other, monster of steel, and he who was known as the Master of Men. And in that moment a queer doubt shook Wentworth. He had termed the thing a robot, as surely it must be, but there was a human mind here... a human mind whose evil reached out to touch him through those blank staring eyes! Wentworth felt the impact, as genuine as a bullet blow, and more dreadful; and he knew what horror it promised for himself, for the humanity which, as the Spider he selflessly served!

Wentworth felt the coldness of his anger mount within him, and while his eyes still gazed at the soulless blank depths of that steel helmet, he spoke in tones of quiet command to Jackson.

"Quickly, Jackson," he snapped. "The First Avenue garage is only a block away. Hurry there and get the heaviest car you can find. This thing is damaged and can't get away very fast! *Hurry, Jackson!*"

Jackson scrambled to his feet, the gun in a shaking hand, but Wentworth knew now that it was anger at his own helplessness that made brave Jackson's hand tremble like that.

"You go, Major," Jackson said hoarsely. "Let me keep watch over this damned thing! You're hurt, and—"

"It is a command, Jackson," Wentworth said quietly. JACKSON FLINCHED as if from a blow, stiffened to attention. "Yes, Major!" he acknowledged. He saluted and whirled to sprint along the street.

Still, Wentworth stared into the blank eyes of the creature of steel. He found an instant then to wonder that there had been no alarm, but he realized the cause instantly. Actually, only a few seconds had elapsed. He was in a neighborhood of wealthy homes whose owners had deserted them for warmer climates at this period of the year. There would be no one here to give an alarm, save guards—and this dead Drexler watchman who lay a score of feet away belonged to the Iron Man!

23

Curiously, Wentworth became aware of Nita's whisper in that silence. Somehow, the Daimler's radio had escaped being wrecked in the crash, and the voice of the woman he loved came to him softly.

"The big blue cat travels fast!" she said, "and takes many kittens with him!"

Wentworth's gray-blue eyes tightened to hardness. The police were already on the way to his home, and they would be swift and thorough. Commissioner Kirkpatrick was his friend, but for that very reason would be the more stern in his execution of justice. Kirkpatrick was a man who served the law with all his strength and keenness—and with all the integrity of his upright soul. If there was stolen loot in his home—and Wentworth had no doubt that it was there—Kirkpatrick would have but one course. Useless to plead that it was a frame-up by criminal foes.

Wentworth shook his head sharply. Damn it, he could not afford to be imprisoned now! Though eventually he might clear himself, those lost hours would mean that he would be out of the war against this monster and his criminal servants—and yet he could not abandon this fight now when he felt it was so nearly won! Let him but charge a car once more against this monster's legs… It was typical of the Spider that he did not even hesitate in his choice. Personal safety, as always, must make way for the demands of the selfless service to which he was pledged!

Abruptly, the robot was in motion. Wentworth stood alertly, waiting for an attack, but the monster ignored him now. Resolutely, the robot turned… toward the wall at the end of the dead-end street! It moved a little awkwardly, and the left leg squeaked a little at every movement. Light slid in glittering contours across the smooth metal back, and it came to Wentworth suddenly that the creature was retreating! But where did it seek to go, when walls lifted on every side?

Wentworth swore and his eyes quested sharply about. Was there nothing he could do to stay the thing's flight? He whipped out his automatic and aimed at the creaking knee joint, pumped out a swift and careful drum-roll of bullets. He could trace the silvery streaks where the bullets struck. They whined off into the night... and the robot did not even turn its head! Fiercely, Wentworth ran toward the shattered traffic standard which had been hurled at him. With a heave of his powerful shoulders he lifted it, and balanced it across straining biceps.

The Spider's face was grimly twisted, for he knew what risk he ran. He had not the strength to hurl this weapon. His only chance was to run with it, like a battering ram. If he missed, if the robot turned at the last moment... Wentworth brushed those considerations from his mind, and began to run, straight toward the monster! At first, his pace was no more than a lumbering trot, but as he gained momentum, his stride lengthened. Finally, he was sprinting at fierce speed with his awkward weapon laid in rest like a spear!

When he was still a dozen feet away, the robot reached the wall at the end of the street. A hand rested against that wall, and there was a muffled concussion! Under the touch of that steel palm, the bricks and mortar fell apart... and the robot stepped through! An instant later, Wentworth crashed his battering ram against the robot's knee, saw a steel hand swoop toward him!

Somehow, Wentworth flung himself backward from the path of that careless blow. The robot's hand caught the iron standard, and plucked it from his grip, sent it tumbling like a stick of kindling across the street... and then the robot walked on into darkness!

AT THE gap in the wall, Wentworth leaned while the breath whistled through his distended nostrils. He was gazing down upon the black, rippling waters of the East River, gazing at the retreating back of the robot. Even as he watched, the monster of steel stepped into the margin of the water... and an instant later, the black flood swallowed it entirely! There was left only a widening ripple in the waters breaking the streaks of reflected light from the stars, from the calm cold moon!

Not suicide, no. The robot had been merely beating a strategic retreat. Wentworth choked down a wild impulse to laughter. Suicide, for a monster of steel? But there was a human brain within it, an inhuman brain... and Kirkpatrick was hurrying toward Wentworth's home to gather up evidence which other servitors of the Iron Man had planted there. By the heavens, this

· NITA VAN SLOAN ·

Iron Man moved swiftly and terribly! And it had a sure and safe retreat beneath the waters of New York harbor!

Wentworth took long steps, that at first were uncertain, along that shattered dead-end street. A moment he stared, and then keenness came into his eyes. If Jackson returned, if he moved swiftly, there might still be a way to defeat the Iron Man's trap and disarm Kirkpatrick's suspicions. Then he could assume the offensive once more, track down these killers....

Grimly, Wentworth bent over the body of the slain watchman. His lips twisted with distaste, but there was no help for the thing he must do. He leaned the man's body against the side of his overturned car, backed away across the street—and fired a single shot! The corpse jerked to the impact of lead, and there was no longer a Spider seal upon his chest! Instead, another wound gaped there beside the one that already had drained his life. An instant later, an auto swerved into the street and Jackson leaped to the pavement.

His voice ran out to Wentworth hoarsely, "Where is it, sir?" he asked.

Wentworth shook his head. "No time for that!" he snapped. "Help me with this body!"

Jackson ran the car to Wentworth's side and, within moments, the body had been placed in the tonneau of the small sedan Jackson had rented. At a word from Wentworth, the car leaped forward, speeding toward his home. This would have to be terribly fast; Kirkpatrick already had been on the way for a couple of minutes and only the fact that Wentworth was nearer his own home than Kirkpatrick gave him any chance at all.

"What's up, sir?" Jackson asked quietly, but there was still strain in his voice, and the muscles made white ridges along his jaw. "God, I hope I never see another thing like that!"

Wentworth's lips parted in a harsh smile. "We're apt to see many more—and battle many more—before this criminal uprising is crushed!" he said swiftly. "I don't know the motive behind this business yet, but it's plain enough that that robot or another like it committed the crimes on Sutton Place! If you could have seen those murdered men...."

"Another like it!" Jackson echoed. "Good God, *more of them!*"

Wentworth made no answer, but his thoughts raced ahead. The dilemma at his home now was a matter of speed. His plans were partly laid, but he had left trouble behind him in the side-street off Sutton Place. The Daimler was wrecked past any removal, and he would have to explain plenty to Kirkpatrick. God in heaven, how could a man explain that monster of steel! But there was a dead policeman back there in the street, and Wentworth's wrecked car....

JACKSON SAID grimly, "I'll double back and... remove that dead cop. Mr. Kirkpatrick won't believe what happened."

Wentworth glanced at Jackson with a smile. As always, Jackson's thoughts were first of the man he served, never of himself. Of what might happen to him if he were caught in his self-assigned task of removing the body of a murdered policeman he made no mention. Wentworth felt a warmth creep through the coldness that had been his heart. By the heavens, with men like this to serve him, he was an ingrate to despair! He would down these robots....

Jackson cried out softly as the car whipped into the side street that flanked Wentworth's Fifth Avenue apartment house, and Wentworth saw the reason why. A long black limousine was just sliding past the street's end, slowing to a halt before the main door—and that limousine had blood-red headlights! It was the car of Stanley Kirkpatrick!

"The private elevator!" Wentworth snapped, and as he spoke, he was stripping off his overcoat, wadding it around his silk hat. "Take this body to the apartment—"

"But the police will come there, sir!"

"Orders, Jackson!" Wentworth snapped. "Listen to me! Take this body to the apartment. In one of the rooms, prob-

ably the music room, you will find
some objects of art that don't belong
there. You will put the fingerprints
of this body on several of them, then
lay it face down beside the doors of
the terrace, or window, with a gun in its hand. Here's his own
gun. Fire that gun a couple of times, and let the bullet marks
show on the wall, but muffle the shots with a wet cloth. Watch
fingerprints! Now, hurry! I'll delay Kirkpatrick!"

As he spoke, he was out of the car, sprinting toward the side
entrance of the apartment building. He raced down the hallway to the main lobby which led past the public elevators to the
front of the building. Through the main doors, closed against the
biting cold of the night, he saw the lean, dapper figure of Kirkpatrick. He was gesturing men into positions about the building! Heaven grant that Jackson already had the body inside the
elevator! Kirkpatrick wheeled then and strode toward the main
doors, and Wentworth ran. He staggered a little, slipping on
the smooth tiled floor, and leaned hard across the information
desk. He shouted toward the man at the telephone switchboard.

"Why in the devil didn't you answer my signal!" he cried. "Get
an ambulance! Get a policeman! Don't sit there staring at me,
call a policeman!"

Wentworth heard the swinging of the outer doors, felt the
gust of cold air that came in with the opening. He pushed
himself back from the counter, whipped out a handkerchief
and mopped his forehead.

"Will you hurry?" he demanded of the still-gaping operator. "I must have a policeman right away!"

Beside him, Kirkpatrick spoke and there was a harder ring than usual to his metallic voice. "Won't I do, Dick?"

Wentworth started violently, then whirled toward his friend and put a smile on his lips. "This is lucky, Kirk," he said energetically. "I—wait a minute. Never mind that call to the police, operator."

The operator shrugged slowly, "What about the ambulance, Mr. Wentworth?" he asked.

WENTWORTH STARED at him as if he did not understand the man. As he figured it, Jackson could not possibly be more than halfway to his penthouse by now. And he had to make the full arrangements before Kirkpatrick reached his apartment. He *had* to! Anything he could do to delay their arrival… "What ambulance?" he asked the operator blankly.

The operator stared in bewilderment and started to explain, but Kirkpatrick cut in sharply. "Dick, I'm waiting for an explanation!"

Wentworth wheeled to face his friend. There was a frown on Kirkpatrick's saturnine countenance, and the mouth beneath the spiked mustache was a harsh line. Wentworth knew he must be careful not to overdo the delay. Kirkpatrick had seen him in too many emergencies for him to believe in any extreme befuddlement.

Wentworth said quietly, "Certainly, Kirk. I'm afraid I'll have to submit to arrest. Technical of course. I just killed a man in my apartment, but—" He massaged his temples. "God, I never saw such a night! First, one of your policemen is killed—"

Kirkpatrick seized him by the arm, "Snap out of it, Dick!" he said fiercely. "What in the devil are you talking about? You've killed a man… Surely, not a policeman!"

Wentworth said, "No, no, I only thought that at first. The man has on a private police agency's uniform. But there is one of your men killed."

Kirkpatrick said violently. "Will you talk sense, Dick? I demand that you give me the whole truth at once! It isn't just luck that I'm here, you know!"

Wentworth said slowly, "Do you want to have someone take down this statement?"

Kirkpatrick started to gesture toward a plainclothesman who had followed him through the doors, then he stared at Wentworth with suddenly narrowed eyes. "We'll take the statement in your apartment," he said sharply. "Come along!"

Wentworth looked at him while his mind raced desperately. Kirkpatrick had seen through his stall, or at least had become suspicious of delay… and Jackson had not yet had time to arrange matters as he had ordered. He shrugged heavily.

"Oh, all right," he said and started toward the elevator, then turned toward the telephone operator. "By the way, if Miss van Sloan should call—"

"Disregard that!" Kirkpatrick snapped at the operator. "By God, Dick, if you're trying any hocus-pocus on me! Why should you come down here to call a policeman? You have two private lines into your home in addition to the one through the switch-board!"

Wentworth faced Kirkpatrick, and there was no smile on his face. "The way you have been behaving lately Kirk," he said shortly, "with your suspicions and persecution of me, I find it expedient to have witnesses for every movement of mine."

Kirkpatrick did not quail under the direct gaze of Wentworth's gray-blue eyes, but a small frown knifed between his brows. "I warn you, Dick," he said quietly, "that every second of delay increases my suspicions of you! I told you it was not luck that I had come here! I have a tip that—"

"That what?" Wentworth demanded as Kirkpatrick broke off.

"That will come later," Kirkpatrick shortly. "Into the elevator at once, or I'll go up without you!"

Wentworth nodded and stepped into the cage. The uniformed man and Kirkpatrick's secretary followed and the elevator sped upward. Wentworth said, wearily, "I suppose I'll have to put up with these suspicions of yours, Kirk, but I warn you they're wearing hard on my liking for you. After all, friendship is based on mutual respect, and really—"

"I'll ask you to account for your movements, Dick," Kirkpatrick interrupted sharply, "from seven o'clock tonight onward!"

"Under the circumstances, perhaps I'd better call my lawyer first," Wentworth snapped, "though I fail to see why I should fall under suspicion for having killed a burglar in my own home! A burglar I tried to capture, and who fired on me twice before I returned a shot!"

"So that's what happened, is it?" Kirkpatrick asked. His voice was utterly without expression.

"Would it be asking too much?" Wentworth went on bitterly, "to demand the reason for your presence, since you would hardly bring your secretary and other officers on a friendly call?"

THE ELEVATOR sighed to a halt, and Kirkpatrick strode out of the cage without reply, jabbed hard at the bell beside Wentworth's door. Wentworth stood idly aside. He had done what he could to delay the police. If Jackson were not ready now, he would have to make a break for it! He peered covertly toward the two men who accompanied Kirkpatrick. Sergeant Reams, the officer in uniform, was not a man who needed orders, otherwise he would not have been Kirkpatrick's bodyguard. He stood by the elevator with a revolver ready in his fist! The door of Wentworth's penthouse opened on the safety chain, and through the opening Wentworth saw the dark bearded face and turbaned head of his other confidential servitor, Ram Singh.

"Open the door," Kirkpatrick ordered brusquely.

Ram Singh's dark eyes regarded Kirkpatrick impassively. "Pardon, Kirkpatrick *sahib*," he said in the deep rumble of his voice, "but do you come in friendship or as the police? If you come as the police…."

Kirkpatrick's anger flushed into his cheekbones, but he checked the angry retort that sprang to his lips. "Confound it, Dick!" he snapped, "there is a reason for these delays!"

"Quite," Wentworth murmured, and his smooth black eyebrows arched in mockery. "The reason lies in your own anger and impatience, for as the Hindus say…" he lapsed into the

Hindustani which Ram Singh understood. *"If all is well, open the door, my comrade. Otherwise, have trouble with the lock.* Which means, Kirk, that the angry man maketh his own impediments."

"Will you order this stubborn Sikh—"Kirkpatrick began, but cut off as the door swung smoothly open.

Ram Singh bowed low, and hid the mockery in his dark gaze, "A thousand pardons, Kirkpatrick *sahib,*"he rumbled. "My turban is in the dust! I did not know that my master accompanied his friend!"

Kirkpatrick strode past him with an oath, and from inside the apartment, Jackson's voice called out calmly, "You came quickly, sir! The body is in here!"

Wentworth followed the angry strides of Kirkpatrick across the drawing room toward the arch that gave into the music chamber beyond, and his quick eyes flashed over the chaste simplicity of the furnishings. He smothered an oath. The body was stretched out as he had ordered upon the floor, and there were bullet scars obviously from the gun in the man's hand… but Wentworth's eyes were fixed on a number of objects placed about the room. They were cleverly disposed, so that they seemed a part of the furnishings, yet Wentworth knew that they were stolen property!

On the grand piano, there was an exquisitely carved Ming vase of moonlight jade, and on the mantel a small antique clock of French fame caught glittering lights with the swing of a pendulum encrusted with precious stones! Surely, the Iron Man, or whoever directed the robot's movements, did not stint for money when he planned a frame-up! Those articles had a value in hundreds of thousands, and their possession might well tempt even a Richard Wentworth to robbery!

Kirkpatrick was standing over the body of the dead man. He reached down to lift the head by the hair, swore softly as he let it fall.

"Your burglar," he said acidly, "is a trusted agent of a private protection agency famed for its integrity. The Drexler agency! But I don't need to tell you that. You know Frank Drexler! Nor do I see that he has stolen anything!"

Wentworth said slowly, "You are quite right, Kirk. It is apparent that this is a most peculiar burglar. He came bearing gifts!" He strolled across the room toward the Ming vase, made a slow business of reaching out for it. "This vase, as I happen to know, being something of a connoisseur in such matters, belongs to one Aaron Smedley, whose house was robbed tonight, and—"

"Don't touch that vase!" Kirkpatrick snapped.

WENTWORTH LET his hand freeze in mid-air, while he turned with lifted brows toward Kirkpatrick. "What have I done now?" he demanded.

Kirkpatrick was standing on braced legs, and his hands were clasped hard behind him. "I do not want your fingerprints on that vase, Dick," he said quietly. *"Unless they are already there!"*

Wentworth shrugged irritably, "Really, Kirk, you're going too far!" He turned angrily across the room. "I insist on an immediate fingerprint test. I have materials here... And would it be asking too much if you also fingerprint the corpse? Or is it a criminal offense for me to make the suggestion?" He continued to fume while he jerked open the drawer of the desk, caught out envelopes of powder, a sufflator, ink pad and papers. "Apparently, you suspect me of robbery! Well, I've confessed homicide. That should satisfy you."

He flung the articles on the desk and Kirkpatrick took them quietly, but Wentworth stood staring down into the drawer. It was only an instant's pause that did not catch the commissioner's attention, but the discovery he made set Wentworth's heart to racing painfully. He had, perhaps, escaped one trap that had been set for him by the fiendish ingenuity of these criminals. It was unlikely Kirkpatrick could contradict the testimony of those fingerprints on the loot. He had hoped to get rid of Kirk now, race on with his investigation—and he had only discovered a second trap! The Iron Man had not been content with planting loot here and tipping the police. The same man who had placed the evidence here had, at the same time, set another snare!

In that drawer, Wentworth habitually kept an automatic registered in his name, and licensed to him. And that gun was gone!

Wentworth had no doubt as to the whereabouts of that gun, or what had been the purpose of the theft. As surely as death itself, that gun was planted now in one of the looted houses; and equally certain, too, was the fact that a bullet would have been fired from it into the mutilated corpse of one of the guards!

A slow and bitter smile disturbed Wentworth's lips. Truly, the Iron Man planned well! Somehow now, he must elude the police, and get to the murder scene before that incriminating gun was found!

Kirkpatrick's voice came to his ears with an accent of relief, but with a reserve that puzzled Wentworth.

"The fingerprints on the vase and clock are undoubtedly those of the dead man," Kirkpatrick said quietly. "Now, Dick, I must ask you to accompany me."

Wentworth turned slowly, and his face was expressionless, but he felt that he knew the answer to this invitation even while he phrased the query, "That's always a pleasure, Kirk," he said, "though I'm a bit weary just now. Would it be impertinent to ask where it is you wish to go?"

Kirkpatrick was unsmiling, too. "I want you to go with me," he said quietly, "to the home of Aaron Smedley."

Wentworth felt the shock of those words and knew that his suspicions were correct. Not only had the gun been planted as he feared—but *Kirkpatrick had been tipped off about that, too!*

Now there was no chance at all of evading Kirkpatrick, of getting there first. He must be with the commissioner when the police found the gun which would pin upon him one of the most atrocious murders the city had known! Against that evidence, the trickery played here would not stand up an instant! Kirkpatrick's keen mind would tell him how he had been tricked. But, damn it, the Spider could not allow himself to be imprisoned! The lives of many of the city's people would be crushed like ants beneath the iron tread of those grim robots, unless the Spider remained at liberty!

Something close to panic goaded Wentworth then, not a fear for himself, but the certainty of the fate that threatened the people he loved and served. Panic....

Wentworth shrugged and, by a violent effort, made his voice easy. "Certainly, Kirk," he agreed. "I will go wearily with you to the home of Aaron Smedley. After that, I hope you will allow me an opportunity to sleep!"

Kirkpatrick's frown refused to lift. "Yes, Dick," he said. "I only hope that you will be allowed to sleep comfortably in your own bed, and not—"

"Not in one of your private guest chambers," Wentworth interrupted with enforced gaiety. "The ones with bars and tool-steel doors!"

CHAPTER 3
THE TRAP IS SPRANG

THROUGH A long moment, the two friends stood face-to-face in the middle of that death-marked music room. The half-angry smile lingered on Wentworth's lips, but Kirkpatrick was completely grave. Wentworth knew that each move the commissioner made against him stabbed Kirkpatrick to the heart; he knew that Kirk would be the more grimly determined to press the evidence against him for that every reason.

Wentworth's mind was racing ahead, canvassing every possibility. Somehow, he had to evade making the trip with Kirkpatrick, arrive before him at the looted home of Aaron Smedley. Not until then could he strike back at these murderous criminals who were, so early in the war, trying to destroy the man they must recognize as their most dangerous enemy! Yes, he must elude Kirkpatrick—but it must be done in such a way that no suspicion attached to him!

Wentworth wheeled abruptly away. "I'll be with you, Kirk, as soon as I change to more appropriate clothing."

Kirkpatrick said, "Certainly… Sergeant Reams, stay in sight of him the entire time."

Wentworth bowed swiftly, but made no demur and accomplished his rapid change under the watchful eyes of Kirkpatrick's bodyguard—and Sergeant Reams kept his revolver in his fist!

Wentworth's stride was crisp with anger as he returned to the music room, clad now in the dark tweeds he preferred, and it put an edge on his voice when he spoke to Kirkpatrick. "As you know," he said, "Nita is always in danger whenever I have been attacked, and I can give no other interpretation to what happened here tonight. You won't mind if I phone her to be careful?"

"No objection," Kirkpatrick told him tonelessly. "You won't mind making the call from this room?"

Wentworth smiled thinly as he swung toward a wall cabinet and removed a portable telephone. He plugged it into a jack in the wall, and went through the routine of dialing a number. He had only one chance of evading Kirkpatrick, and that would draw Nita into danger as well as himself. There was no other way… and he had plugged the telephone into a radio circuit instead of the regular phone line. That very action would start the transmitter on the roof into operation. He could only hope that Nita would be listening….

"Nita, dear?" he threw his voice into the air. "I'm glad I caught you at home. Yes, I'm at home, too. I wish you were here!" He emphasized that phrase very slightly. If Nita heard, she would know what he meant, and she would get here as quickly as possible. "No, unfortunately, I have to go out again. Kirkpatrick has invited me most urgently."

Kirkpatrick said shortly, "Cut that short, Dick! You wanted to warn her!"

Wentworth's shoulder tautened at the peremptory tone. Kirkpatrick must indeed be on edge. He made no response, continued to speak into the blankness of the air. If only he could be sure Nita was listening!

"Dear, I want you to take particularly good care of yourself. Keep your gun always handy. Yes, I've been attacked once tonight by this new criminal gang, and that means danger... to you, dear. Yes, of course, I'll be careful. I'm always ready for any unexpected events that may develop. As you say it is the unexpected thing that is demoralizing. You know the Hindustani proverb?"

Kirkpatrick's heel thudded on the floor. "You will confine yourself to English, Dick!" he snapped.

Wentworth turned deliberately to face him, and it was in English that he spoke into the transmitter. He already had conveyed most of his message to Nita. She must come to him at once. He had mentioned his gun, and said he had been attacked; that he would be ready for 'unexpected events.'

"As the Hindus say," he went on, " 'In peace, the thunder of chariots goes unheard; in war, the rattle of a small sword startles an army.' Yes, of course dear, I'll see you soon. The first moment I am free. I have to leave now with Kirk. Goodnight!"

WENTWORTH HUNG up slowly, jerked out the plug lest Kirkpatrick understand how he had sent out that message. If Nita had heard him, he had no doubt that she would understand his double speech. If she would only 'rattle a small sword' he would have a chance to escape from Kirkpatrick!

Wentworth accepted his coat and hat from Ram Singh, laid his gaze upon the Sikh and Jackson. "You two will remain here pending further orders," he said curtly. "Do you mind, Kirk, if I tell them to send my lawyers over to headquarters if I have not returned in a few hours?"

Kirkpatrick said grimly, "Not at all, Dick. If you have not returned in a few hours, your lawyers will be needed!"

The eyes of the two men met in challenge and it was only Wentworth who smiled, albeit grimly. He buttoned his coat deliberately pulled the soft brim of his felt over his brows. He had done what he could to meet this crisis. If Nita had not heard him, there would have to be another attempt, regardless of whether it aroused Kirkpatrick's suspicions still more. He must recover that gun before it fell into the hands of the police!

"I'm ready, Kirk," he said quietly.

Kirkpatrick nodded, motioned to Sergeant Reams and they filed out together. Wentworth was conscious of Jackson's eyes on him appealingly, of the smoldering anger that Ram Singh barely suppressed. His two men were ready to hurl themselves upon the police at any cost. They did not know what threatened, but that he was in danger was abundantly clear—and yet he had ordered them to remain behind! But it was necessary. If Nita obeyed his suggestion, there must be no added danger to her sweet life!

As they crossed the first floor lobby, Wentworth glanced covertly at his watch and saw that almost five minutes had elapsed since he had first spoken to Nita. It was time enough for her to reach here… if she had heard! At the entrance, Wentworth tucked a cigarette between his lips and, just outside, he paused to flick flame to his lighter. He had a little trouble so that Kirkpatrick and Sergeant Reams passed him, turned stiffly to keep him under constant surveillance. Wentworth got the cigarette lighted, slowly pocketed the lighter… and still nothing happened. Had Nita then failed to get his message?

"Come on, Dick," Kirkpatrick urged impatiently. "I've never seen you so dilatory as tonight." He jerked open the door of the big limousine, motioned Wentworth inside. Sergeant Reams flanked the door on the other side, gun in his fist. Wentworth caught the sigh that pushed to his teeth. He would have no choice then but to make a break for it, to try and conciliate Kirkpatrick afterward. He settled the brim of his hat more firmly about his brows—and heard the squeal of skidding auto tires!

Wentworth stiffened at the sound. Out of his eye corners he saw a battered coupé sweep around the corner from beside the apartment house. The window nearest him was down and, even as he peered that way, he caught the silhouette of a slouch hat pulled low over the driver's brows. And then gun-flame blossomed from that dark interior! Lead screamed over his head and smashed through the glass in the door behind him!

Then he had his own automatic
out and was sprinting
toward the coupé.

A shout sprang to Wentworth's lips, a shout of exultation! Nita had heard him and understood! Wentworth changed the cry to surprise, to fright. He went down on one knee, and two more of Nita's bullets slammed overhead! Then he had his own automatic out and was sprinting toward the coupé! It had straightened out of the skidding turn and was darting across Fifth Avenue. Out of his eye corners, Wentworth caught sight of Sergeant Reams. He had dropped to his knee behind a fire-hydrant and the light gleamed coldly on his revolver. Kirkpatrick wheeled stiffly beside the limousine and the long-barreled .38 with which he was so expert was ready in his hand. Good God! If those two marksmen opened up on Nita....

WENTWORTH SHOUTED fiercely. "Come on, Kirk! They're the crooks who tried to frame me! In that coupé!" He hurled himself forward in a violent sprint—straight into the line of fire of the two officers!

Wentworth heard Kirkpatrick cry out harshly, felt the breeze of lead streaking past his head... and knew that he had disconcerted the aim of the police! Wentworth's own gun was kicking in his hand, but he was throwing his lead deliberately high. Half-way across Fifth Avenue, he shouted his challenge back to Kirkpatrick.

"Come on! I got a tire on that coupé! We'll run it down!"

He put everything he had into a hard sprint, heard Kirkpatrick's feet thud against the pavement behind him, heard his order to Sergeant Reams to "follow with the car!" As if to put a period to his sentence, one final shot blasted from the coupé before it whipped out of sight—and there was a hissing explosion followed by the sharp curse of Sergeant Reams. Nita, bless her cool courage and intelligence, had fully grasped the situation. She had shot a tire of Kirkpatrick's car!

Kirkpatrick was fifteen yards behind when Wentworth rounded the corner into the side street. By the end of the next block, where the coupé, wobbling as if from a punctured tire, had turned, Wentworth had increased that lead to fifty yards. He heard Kirkpatrick call out breathlessly but answered only with a shout.

"Come on!" he cried. "We're gaining!"

Around that corner, the coupé was motionless at the curb, the door flung wide! With a long bound, Wentworth was on the running board and instantly the coupé lurched forward. Nita's quick, excited laughter was warm.

"How do you like me as a torpedo, Dick?" she cried, still laughing gaily.

The coupé whipped around the next corner and streaked on into the night. Briefly, street lights shone upon the smooth oval of Nita's face, glistened on her shining eyes. The tendrils of her chestnut curls twisted out from beneath the confines of the man's hat she had tugged low over her brows. She looked like a child at an amusing prank, but Wentworth knew what fears throbbed in her breast for him. It was part of the compact between them, the oath they had sworn when Wentworth had lost his fight against their love and told her the truth of his harried existence, and the fact that they could never marry while work remained for the Spider! She would never show her fears....

Wentworth mastered his pumping lungs, and his hand was

gentle upon her shoulders. "Eastward, dear, and fast," he said. "Stop near the first taxi you see… Sweet, you took too much chance back there, more than was necessary."

Nita shook her head, and there was deviltry about the tender curve of her lips. "It had to be realistic Dick. Is anything less than that worthy of… the Spider's true love?"

Wentworth laughed softly. "I think you'll have to stop the car," he said.

Nita's face was immediately sober. She glanced to the rear and asked sharply, "Are we followed?"

Wentworth shook his head, "No, but I doubt if even the Spider's true love can drive efficiently while being kissed!"

It was only an instant's pause on a dark side-street, halfway between danger and despair; then the coupé once more was boring through the night while Wentworth hurriedly explained the things that had happened this night; the things that still threatened to happen.

"Without a doubt, dear," Wentworth rushed on, "Kirkpatrick must have thrown a strong guard about those houses on Sutton Place the instant he received the tip about the murder gun being there. But he will want to make the search in person. As soon as I leave you—there's a taxi parked ahead, I'll take that—phone Jackson to get out of the building without being seen. He is to proceed at once to Sutton Place, put on the robes of the Spider and, when he sees me talking to the police guards, he will show himself long enough to draw those guards away!"

NITA DREW in a slow breath. "The peril must be very great, Dick, for you to assign risky jobs to anyone except yourself!"

Wentworth's arm closed hard about Nita's shoulders as she eased the coupé to a halt. "Greater than anyone could realize who has not seen those robots, if that's what the thing was," he said grimly. "Heaven grant, dear, that you never come in contact with them. If you do… If you do run as fast as you can! Nothing can stop them!"

The coupé halted, and Wentworth swept Nita once more into his arms. She was so small, so soft, in his powerful embrace; so vulnerable. Those monsters in steel… His arms tightened. "When you've transmitted those orders, go to my home," he said. "You should be safe with Ram Singh to guard you. And—be careful, dear!"

Nita's lips trembled under his caress, but her voice came out clearly, even with a hint of laughter. "Certainly," she said. "It is a lesson we have learned from you! Always to be careful of ourselves!"

There was time for no more of these sweets stolen from a life of perpetual peril, of feverish battles. Wentworth flung around the corner, and sprang into the taxi, tossed a Sutton Place address at the driver. When he peered back, he saw Nita's brave figure turning into the corner drug store. Within a few minutes, Jackson would be receiving his orders….

There was a grim tautness in the thrust of Wentworth's jaw as he tore his thoughts away from Nita and her peril. His ruse had succeeded against Kirkpatrick. Within a few minutes now, he would recover that stolen automatic and then he could turn his attentions to the criminals who struck such shrewd and wanton blows against him. This was a battle that must be joined and settled quickly. He could not permit such creatures as these robots to range at the will of criminals. The potentialities for awful slaughter were too great. And already, he had had proof enough that the will for slaughter existed! Those four poor devils in the homes on Sutton Place....

A block from the looted homes, Wentworth paid off the cab and sauntered into an all-night drug store where he put through a call for his own apartment house, had the operator page Kirkpatrick. Within moments, the stormy voice of the commissioner blasted over the wire!

"Where are you, Dick?" he demanded. "By God, you ran out on me, and—"

"I trailed the coupé in a cab," Wentworth said crisply, "but the beggar got away from me finally on the upper East Side. I'm at Sutton Place now, where I expected you'd already be. Shall I wait for you here?"

Wentworth heard Kirkpatrick's smothered oath over the wire. "You will go at once and place yourself in the custody of the first policeman you see," Kirkpatrick ordered. "There are twenty stationed around the looted houses on Sutton Place. At once, you understand, Dick? It is now three-fourteen. You will make that surrendered by three-sixteen."

Wentworth's voice rasped angrily into the transmitter. "This one time I'm taking orders, Kirk," he snapped. "Hereafter, you will come to see me on official business only!"

HE SLAMMED the receiver into its hook and swung out of

the phone booth. His eyes were narrowed and hard. He could not blame Kirkpatrick for doing his full duty, but it seemed to him that the commissioner was too quick at accepting anonymous information against a friend. The tips could have been only anonymous. Wentworth shook his head, bowed into the bitter wind that moaned along Sutton Place.

The sky was overcast now, and only the transient beams from the street lights relieved the shadows. He saw the policemen ringed about the three buildings where the murders had occurred, and moved steadily toward them. A dozen blocks farther along was the dead-end street where he had battled the robot. But these police must have been thrown about the houses since that time. Had the murder of the policeman been reported?

At the memory, Wentworth stopped sharply in his tracks. Jackson had said he would remove that body and Wentworth had given no countermanding of that determination. Jackson might well have concluded that his instructions to remain at home had been given for Kirkpatrick's ears alone. In that case, there would be no diversion created here to permit his entrance. But he could not turn back now. Kirkpatrick had given him only two minutes, and the police guard had already seen him approaching.

Wentworth sent his sharp gaze stabbing ahead, picked out the facade of Aaron Smedley's home. That was the most logical place for the planting of his gun, since the loot left in his apartment had come from that home. He must surrender to the police, yet elude them to recover that gun—and do it in a space

51

of minutes. Kirkpatrick would be in furious haste to arrive now that he knew Wentworth was already here.

Wentworth walked straight up to the nearest policeman, nodded to him pleasantly. "I'm meeting Kirkpatrick here," he said quietly. "I believe he'll be here in a few minutes."

The policeman lifted his nightstick in salute. "Yes, sir," he agreed. "A bitter night to be on duty."

Wentworth nodded absently, and leaned his hips against the iron fence which surrounded the basement well of the Smedley house. Minutes, and then Kirkpatrick would he here. His own course was clear. He would have to absent himself, take a chance on allaying Kirkpatrick's suspicions....

"Too cold," he agreed. "When the commissioner arrives, tell him I'm waiting in the bar room over there on the corner."

Wentworth nodded, started across the street and then an oath sprang to his lips. He muffled it, kept deliberately on his way. It was not for him to call attention to that grim silhouette on the roof of the buildings across the street, a figure of hunched shoulders, draped in a long cape—a silhouette which any of the police, and half the populace of the city would recognize instantly, and....

Wentworth whipped about as a policeman lifted a hoarse shout: "Look! Hey, get him! Look, on the roof there—*the Spider!*"

There was that moment's pause while the man's frightened shout ran down the street, and then there was a concerted crash of gunfire! Even then the figure on the roof did not immediately dodge back out of sight. It stood peering down into the dark canyon of the street, the black cape sweeping out on the breath of the wind. Wentworth's teeth set fiercely. Why didn't Jackson get back out of range? He had exposed himself long enough now. He—instead of retreating, the caped figure suddenly whipped out a gun and emptied it in a swift drum roll which shattered windows in the Smedley house behind Wentworth! Then it turned and ran lightly along the front ridge of the roofs across the street!

THE POLICE went past Wentworth in a blue flood, their voices as fierce as the bay of hounds that rush in to the kill. Wentworth hesitated, while his eyes followed that flitting figure with the cape kiting at its shoulders. This was not like Jackson, to expose himself needlessly to gun fire. What was necessary he would do, but beyond that he was too wise a man, too experienced with guns and the carnage they wrought to take useless chances. Wentworth shook his head at the sudden, frightened thought that crossed his mind. He could hear, through the hammer of furiously released police guns, the thin distant wailing of a siren. It meant that Kirkpatrick was on the way; that Wentworth had only a few moments left to seize the chance which the Spider masquerade afforded him. But fear was still there in his heart as he darted, unobserved by the preoccupied police, through the smashed windows of the Smedley house! The figure of the Spider had seemed so small. But this was madness. It could not be... *Nita!*

Wentworth told himself that, as he quested swiftly through the lower floor of the Smedley house, but his mind was distracted. If Jackson had left on his self-appointed errand, this was exactly what Nita would do; come herself in the masquerade of the Spider! God, he had to make this fast! It would be just like Nita to continue the diversion until she saw Wentworth emerge safely from the beleaguered house! Wentworth's pocket flash eagerly probed the room, glittered on the smashed shards of art treasures which the killers had left. Wanton vandalism. Staring at the wreckage, Wentworth could see the work of the steel flails which were the arms of robots. Anger shook him. He sent the flashlight toward the window portieres… and it glinted on his gun! With a glad cry, he sprang toward it.

Outside, the hammer of guns went on, and the shriek of the siren was louder. When he reappeared, the false Spider could flee. Wentworth stooped swiftly toward the gun… and it was only belatedly that his caution returned to him. He remembered then that his light had passed this spot once before, and that on the previous occasion the gun had not been here!

Even as the significance of that fact flashed across his mind, he hurled himself toward the portieres while his left hand clawed for the heavy automatic that nested beneath his arm. He was too late. Before his hand could close on the gun, before he could touch the portieres, he saw a hand snake out from behind the curtain and a blackjack swung viciously toward his skull!

Brilliant lights exploded within Wentworth's skull, and he pitched to the floor. There was agony in his brain, but all his senses were terribly acute. He tried to drive strength into his limbs, and he could not move at all. But he could hear with a clarity that seemed to give him a new vision. Feet moved softly toward him. There was a thin snickering laughter just above his head, and then the chill touch of steel in the palm of his right hand. After that, only the clatter of guns and the mounting shriek of the siren.

Wentworth knew what had happened all right. That was the damnable part of the thing. His brain was startlingly clear, though he could move not even a finger. The crook, perhaps the leader himself of this dread combination of horror and robbery, had hidden here to make sure that the incriminating gun was not removed before the police were at hand. Wentworth, his mind concentrated on his fears for Nita, had walked into the trap. He would lie here unconscious now, and the gun beneath his hand was a murder weapon!

"Now," he heard that hateful voice just above him whisper. "Now, the Spider will walk no more!"

CHAPTER 4
ON THE SPOT

A LESSER man than the Spider would have fought through brief seconds against the benumbing effects of that blow and, failing, would have been doomed. Wentworth's body was defeated, but his mind fought on; his will was a flame of naked steel. That siren dinned dimly in his ears, and the Spider commanded his body to rise.

Perspiration broke out on his forehead under the assault of his will. The muscles of his legs and arms twitched, and there was no strength in them. But it was the will of the Master of Men that commanded. There was that moment of pause and then, slowly, as if each individual limb weighed a ton, Wentworth's arm drew beneath him. His legs tensed—and the Spider staggered to his feet!

There was no feeling in his legs, and his head sagged like a broken thing. He moved and his feet scuffed the floor in the dragging step of a paralytic. He stood there in that dark room and forced his head up. His hands still gripped the gun, his soft hat was on his head. The siren shrieked furiously in the street, and the gunshots were dying. There was so little time; so little.

The window would not serve now. He could not thrust his crippled body through it. The door... It swung open under the grip of Wentworth's gloved hand. He stumbled out into the shadows of the portico, somehow reached the sidewalk. Kirkpatrick's car blazed past toward where the police were grouped excitedly in the street. Their eyes were turned upward, but the silhouette of the Spider no longer showed there on the skyline. Fear like physical pain thrust through Wentworth's heart. What had happened then? Had Nita....

He smothered the thought. Every shred of his concentrated will was necessary even to achieve movement. Close in the shadow of the building, he turned away from the police and presently angled toward the other side; toward the bar room where he had told the policeman he would wait. Thoughts drove through his brain like individual spikes. His will was the sledge. Kirkpatrick must not see him come from the direction of the Smedley home. Beyond that, he could not plan now.

He reached the center of the street, sought for no more. He turned then and moved toward Kirkpatrick's car. The cold stab of the wind was grateful in his lungs. He felt that presently the curtain of numbness that had dropped over his brain would lift, but not yet. Not yet. He forced his head erect, tried to put briskness in his stride, but twice he stumbled where there was no obstacle at all. His pain-squeezed eyes reached ahead to where Kirkpatrick's lean, military figure stood beside the big red-eyed limousine and shouted orders. Evidently, he asked some question about Wentworth, for one of the policeman lifted a pointing arm and Kirkpatrick pivoted sharply about to stare where Wentworth walked.

Steady, Wentworth cautioned himself: *Put your feet down briskly and keep your bearing jaunty...* If Kirkpatrick discovered he had been slugged, it was tantamount to admitting that he had entered the guarded building. The gun... good God! He still had the gun in his pocket! Too late now to do anything about it. **KIRKPATRICK'S VOICE** came crisply: "Where have you been?" he demanded. "I told you to surrender yourself to the nearest policeman!"

Wentworth tried to answer and his tongue moved thickly in his mouth.

"Well?" Kirkpatrick snapped.

Wentworth managed to shrug. His words lacked their usual precise delivery. "I... waited," he mumbled. He nodded toward the officer with whom he had spoken previously. "Officer will tell you."

Kirkpatrick frowned, and the policeman grinned slightly as he peered toward Wentworth. "Right, sir. He was with me when the Spider was sighted...."

"With you?" Kirkpatrick demanded.

"Right with me," the policeman nodded. "The gentleman said he would wait for you in the bar around the corner. I… think he did!" The cop hid another grin, and Kirkpatrick glared sharply at Wentworth.

It was the cue which Wentworth had awaited. He laughed loudly. "Right," he said. "Did wait in the bar. Good lord, that last drink packed an awful wallop. Went right to my head!"

Kirkpatrick did not smile. He looked at Wentworth, but his words were addressed to the policeman beside him. "You were standing right in front of the Smedley house when the Spider was sighted, I take it," he said.

"Yes, Commissioner."

"You left this gentleman with free access to the Smedley house, officer?"

The red crept up the policeman's cheeks. "Why, yes, sir. The gentleman was waiting for you, and the Spider—"

Kirkpatrick's laughter was sharp, triumphant. "Exactly! Officer O'Holian, *search this man!*"

The command fell like a shock across Wentworth's mind, and the veil of pain finally lifted, though his head still reeled from a blow which would have rendered a lesser man unconscious for an hour. He stiffened at Kirkpatrick's words, and he took a step backward. He seemed merely indignant, but he was frantic. With that murder gun in his pocket, he dared not submit to search! There was no longer any doubt that Kirkpatrick had been told in detail what evidence he would find in the Smedley home.

"This has gone far enough, Kirkpatrick!" Wentworth said harshly. "You presume upon friendship!"

Kirkpatrick motioned the policeman forward. "You are wrong, Dick," he said. "No malefactor is my friend! If you have nothing incriminating upon you, you cannot object to search! Now then, permit the officer to do his duty!"

Wentworth faced the policeman squarely. "I have not been arrested," he warned the man. "You have no right to search me, and I will not submit." His words were quiet, but the cold force of the voice of the Master of Men struck through his tone. The policeman checked, but Wentworth recognized that this was only a momentary respite. Kirkpatrick would insist. He had to find a way out. Had to! If the murder gun were found, he would no longer be able to fight against the Iron Man and his criminal cohorts… Wentworth reckoned grimly that the Iron Man would have a terrific score to settle when this was finished!

"You have illusions of grandeur," Wentworth snapped at Kirkpatrick, and his voice rose. He was stalling desperately for time. He had only one slim chance… if Jackson or Nita were within sound of his voice. If he could make them understand what he wanted, he might still evade Kirkpatrick. Yes, a slim chance.

"This is America, and there is a constitution to protect my rights!" he declared. "God in heaven, haven't I been through enough tonight? An attempt to frame me in my home. *I have even been shot at in the street!*

"Do you think criminals want me dead because I have *helped* them? *At any minute, there may be another attack on my life!*"

Kirkpatrick said drily, "I hardly think it possible with all these police around you. Enough of this—"

WENTWORTH LAUGHED harshly. "There were police around me last time I was shot at! A bullet can come from any shadow... But that is beside the point, merely a proof of my innocence. His words rang clearly. *I would rather be shot than submit to the indignity of such a search!*"

Had his words been heard, Wentworth wondered desperately? He dared not make his meaning clearer—and there was always the possibility that Jackson, or brave Nita if it had been she in the disguise of the Spider, had been wounded. Kirkpatrick gestured impatiently.

"You will either submit to search here and now," he said shortly, "or you will be taken to police headquarters on charges of suspicion of murder! Take your choice!"

Wentworth said, stiffly, "The choice is easy!" He could not stall much longer. It was clear none of his comrades was within the sound of his voice. Better to make a run for it, and....

The sound of the shot that was fired from an opposite roof was loud in the waiting silence of the street. The tongue of flame reached downward fiercely.

Wentworth blew out his breath in a thin whisper of sound and pitched limply forward to the street. For an instant, there was only shocked silence in the street, and then bedlam broke loose. A half dozen police guns blasted toward the roof ambuscade, but Kirkpatrick cried out and dropped on his knees beside Wentworth. He bent close over him... and it gave Wentworth the chance he sought. The incriminating gun already was in his hand. As Kirkpatrick bent toward him, his back was toward Wentworth's right hand… and Wentworth whipped the gun toward a street sewer opening a dozen feet away!

Through the racket of the street, he heard the gun rasp on metal, and knew that it had struck the grating accurately. It was a sound that would go unnoticed in the general clamor.

"Play up," he whispered to Kirkpatrick. "If the killer thinks he got me, he'll stop shooting!"

Kirkpatrick swore and ripped to his feet. "Faking!" The commissioner glared down at Wentworth irresolutely through a long moment then turned to peer up toward the roof from which the shot had come. Wentworth seized that opportunity to glance toward the sewer opening, and an oath sprung to his lips. The gun had struck the grating all right. But it still hung there, balanced on the edge of the grating, and to Wentworth it seemed that all light in the street concentrated on the exposed butt!

He sprang to his feet, and Kirkpatrick whipped toward him. His call brought O'Holian back to his side. "Once before, Dick," he said quietly, "you escaped my custody during gunplay. I am making no accusation—"

"I should be thankful, I suppose!" Wentworth mocked.

"—but my ultimatum holds good!" Kirkpatrick pressed on. "Submit to search, or you go to jail!"

Wentworth met Kirkpatrick's frosty glare through a long moment, then slowly he lifted his hands. "Very well," he said grimly, "but I think you'll regret this, Kirkpatrick!"

Kirkpatrick's face was rigid as frozen earth. There was both determination and a wincing dread in his expression. "It is possible," he said heavily. "O'Holian, get on with the search!"

While the policeman made his rapidly thorough search, Wentworth allowed his eyes to stray covertly toward the sewer opening. A uniformed man was sauntering that way. If he should catch sight of that gun-butt... Wentworth shifted impatiently.

"It might help O'Holian, Kirk," he said shortly, "if you would tell him what he's looking for."

"A thirty-eight caliber automatic," Kirkpatrick said grimly. "A colt, with a test barrel."

"It ain't on him, sir," O'Holian reported steadily. "His gun is a forty-five, and he's got a license for it here."

Kirkpatrick's whole body seemed to relax, though his voice remained toneless. "Very well, O'Holian," he said. "That will do." WENTWORTH SAW that the policeman had reached the sewer. He was kicking the metal grating absently with his toe. How could he help seeing that gun butt? "If you're through with your insults," he said stiffly. "I'm going home." His mind was very active.

Kirkpatrick nodded gravely. His frosty blue eyes were puzzled, but there was suffering in their depths. Actually, he detested these moments when he had to accuse his friend. Things would be a little smoother, now, with the searching over and done—if only... Wentworth turned aside and glanced once more toward the policeman. He was standing on the grating now, staring up at the front of the Smedley house. His toes were almost touching the dangling gun!

A grim smile touched Wentworth's lips. It was a time for

hairline measures! He turned excitedly toward Kirkpatrick, pointed toward the policeman.

"What is that man's name?" he demanded.

Kirkpatrick frowned. "Patrolman Kelly," he growled, "but what—"

"*Kelly!*" Wentworth called sharply. "Here at once!"

As he had calculated, the man started at the sudden summons. He executed a neat about face... and his toe brushed the gun, sent it spinning down into the sewer! Wentworth blew out a relieved sigh, but masked it. He peered hard into the face of the policeman. He shook his head, puzzled.

"I could have sworn, from the set of this man's shoulders," he said slowly, "that he was the driver of that coupé that got away from me tonight, but I got a glimpse of the man's face, and it wasn't Kelly. I'm sorry."

Kirkpatrick said sharply, "Do you think the police harbor assassins?"

Wentworth looked him directly in the eye, "It is peculiar," he said slowly, "that both times I've been fired on tonight, it has been after police brought me out into the open!"

Kirkpatrick started an angry answer, but cut off the words before he began them. "You are at liberty to go, Dick," he said slowly. "I... I bear you no ill feeling, man, but you must realize I can show no favoritism in the execution of my duty!"

Wentworth was torn. He wanted nothing more than to grip

firmly the hand that Kirkpatrick half extended, but friendship with the commissioner was becoming too hampering. There was a titan's battle ahead, and he must throw off all handicaps.

Instead of taking the half-proffered hand then, Wentworth bowed stiffly, swung on his heel and strode away. There was no time for personal grief. He must hurl himself at once into the fray, where he had been forced to leave off to avoid the traps of the Iron Man's hirelings. As he stalked toward the corner bar, his eyes quested once more, and vainly, over the building from which the shots had come. There, a few minutes ago, the Spider had flaunted his robes at the police. Heaven grant that his substitute had not been trapped!

Wentworth cut into the bar room, angled at once toward a corner phone booth. There was only one party in the narrow dining room behind the bar, two men and women noisily jubilant over their drinks. Wentworth ignored them to shoot through a call to his home. Now, in a few minutes, he would learn the truth. If Jackson had left earlier, then it had been Nita who had worn the Spider's garb!

His call went through swiftly, and in a few moments, Ram Singh's harsh voice rasped over the line.

"Orders, Ram Singh," he snapped. "In my stores is a rubber diving suit with a helmet and oxygen tank. Get a fresh tank of oxygen and rush the equipment to Sutton Place. Understood?"

"Han, sahib!" Ram Singh echoed deeply. "Fortunate it is that thy servant obeyed his orders. That foolish braggart, Jackson, left almost as soon as thyself, and...."

WENTWORTH'S FACE hardened at this confirmation

of his guess. Jackson had gone to remove the body of the policeman from the dead-end street, and Nita… Nita had worn the Spider's robes!

"He went to risk his life for our honor, Ram Singh," Wentworth said gently. "Hurry, thou mighty warrior!"

Twice, he groped for the hook while his unseeing eyes stared straight before him. Once more, he was seeing that bravely daring figure flaunt defiance at the police, so small in the black and ominous robes of the Spider. God, if anything had happened to her… Wentworth thrust at the door of the booth, and the fatigue of his strenuous night hit him all at once. The throbbing of his head seemed to swell. He stumbled as he moved toward the bar, and ordered a brandy. He could not search for her, not now, lest the police follow him….

At his elbow, a voice spoke, "How about buying us a drink, big boy?"

Wentworth started and whirled. *"Nita!* he cried.

Nita was leaning her elbows on the bar beside him, and there was mockery in the gay smile that curved her lips. "So this is how you spend your spare time," she chided him. "I'm afraid, Dick, that you will be far from a model husband!"

Wentworth's hands gripped hers hard, and his eyes drank in the laughter in the violet depths of her gaze. "You come out of here, young lady," he ordered. "You and I are going to have a talk!"

Nita laughed, tucked her hand under his arm, and they were almost at the door when the barkeep returned with Wentworth's drink. The man swore, then shrugged and tossed the drink off himself.

"Quickest pickup I ever saw," he nodded confidentially to himself in the mirror.

But Wentworth was not even aware he had spoken. He had no need of brandy, with Nita at his side, and he turned under her direction toward the coupé which she had parked two blocks away.

"You're taking too many chances, dear," he told Nita sternly. "Though in this instance I'll admit it was fortunate for me that you did. Nevertheless, you go home now as fast as I can ship you there!"

Nita shook her head in mock bitterness, though there was worry in her violet eyes. "That's the thanks I get for coming to you," she said. "I'm just beginning to enjoy myself!"

Wentworth smiled down upon her. "You're fired," he told her grimly. His heart swelled at recognition of her bravery, for he knew that she was torn with terror for him; for the battle that lay ahead. As always, she thought not of herself, but of cheering him. Her hand clung to his now.

"Dick, surely now you can rest," she said. "Just for tonight—"

Wentworth jerked his head in negation. He said, "In this battle, every passing hour means more deaths! I'll take you to a taxi, and then—"

"And then?" Nita's question was no more than a breath.

"Why then," Wentworth said softly, "I shall hunt for robots! I have a theory about those monsters, and if I'm right it will be possible to stop them. I hope so, and—"

He broke off then as they stopped beside the coupé, for a man had suddenly darted around the nearby corner. Wentworth's hand flicked toward his automatic, but the man did not come toward them, did not even seem to see them. His breath rasped in his throat and he ran heavily, as a man would run at the extreme end of exhaustion. His shoulder struck a light post, and he reeled aside, but did not check his pace at all. He rounded another corner and was gone.

Nita said, "He looked… frightened!"

WENTWORTH WHIPPED open the door of the coupé and thrust Nita inside and there was grim tension on his face. As he ducked in behind the wheel, he heard a woman's cry soar up desolately into the night. It was a hoarse cry, more animal than human in its intensity. Nita shuddered.

"In heaven's name, Dick," she whispered. "What can be happening?"

Wentworth said, "I hope I'm wrong. I hope to heaven I'm wrong!"

He sent the car surging forward, careened around the corner from which the man had spurted. Immediately ahead, the street was empty, but even as they sped forward, some people burst into sight from a side-way. They were running desperately. The night swallowed them. The sound of their pounding feet was drowned out in a rumbling crash that spread its thunder like a tangible weight upon the air. The windshield of the coupé jarred with concussion, and afterward there were mounting, ghastly screams! The roar of mingled voices became a vast murmur of fear and horror.

Wentworth said, with difficulty, "I was right. The robots are marching!"

As if his words had brought forth the sound, a new rhythm in the paean of terror began to make itself felt, more than heard. It was even, deep as primitive drums, as if giant clubs were used to turn the earth itself into a drum. It was slow, with a heavy insistent rhythm; slow as a funeral dirge, but more ominous. It continued as Wentworth drove the coupé around another corner, and the scene burst upon his eyes.

At first, there was only the wildly terrified flight of people. They were in all stages of undress. Children screamed their fright as they ran barefooted across the freezing pavements; women raced with backward twisted faces and streaming hair, some falling, to rise and run again. A running man collided with another and lashed out at the other frenziedly. His blow fell viciously low in the body. The man he had struck did not check. He ran on, bent agonizingly forward, holding his body and still running. He did not even look at the man who had hit him.

In an instant, the street was blocked with the fleeing scores of people, and once more the Spider and Nita van Sloan heard the thunderous reverberation.

"Dick!" Nita gasped, and her voice was strained. "Dick, do you realize what they're doing! They're—they're pushing over buildings! Buildings in which people live! That must have been a huge tenement…."

The screams of the new victims were tossed up like sparks in the hot breath of a holocaust. Beside the car, a woman with a child in her arms tripped over the curb and fell! In an instant, she was buried under the rush of other people. Her cries rose weakly, but she was given no chance to regain her feet! The child wailed... With an oath, Wentworth flung himself from the stalled coupé. Men collided with him as insensately as if he was a post. He had to fight furiously to divide the stampede so that he could reach the woman. She crouched miserably upon the pavement, elbows and knees on the concrete while she sheltered the child beneath her. In those few brief moments, her clothing had been torn almost from her; her left hand had been ground to a pulp.

Wentworth slammed his fists about him, knocked men aside and stooped to help the woman to her feet. His hands were gentle despite the stampede which in an instant had swept them past the coupé and into the eddy behind it. He placed the child in her arms.

The woman did not speak. Her drawn face peered once back the way she had come and then she was plunging on with the crowd, the child clasped in her arms. It was a fight to regain the side of the coupé. Wentworth flung himself to its top, stared down the dark way the people had come and, as he stared, he felt the strained pallor creep into his cheeks. The funereal rhythm was all about him, was palpable in the air. Heavy and slow and awful in its suggestion of power. For that single moment, Wentworth could see nothing... and then the drumbeat of fury was louder, was in the street itself. He was gazing at the glimmering steel helmets of an entire squad of robots. It was the ground-trembling impact of their steel-shod feet that he had heard!

CHAPTER 5
"LOCK ON THE HELMET"

E VEN AS he stared, two of the robots detached themselves from the squad and pivoted to the left. Their hands reached out—and the entire front wall of a small tenement gave way before their pressure! Falling brick rained down upon their steel-clad heads; collapsing walls lapped like furious waters about their inhuman legs. When the job was done, they turned and walked out of the debris as a man would wade a brook, and behind them people screamed in discovery of fresh horror. Wentworth saw a child dangling from the broken edge of a high floor; saw that hold slip....

Eight steel monsters there were, swinging in a formal squad in the midst of destruction. Those who lingered in their path, died. The careless clash of steel feet, the swing of beam-like arms brushed human beings from their paths like flies, and always there was that awful, overbearing rhythm, the dirge-like crunch of those awful feet!

Wentworth found that his automatic was in his fist and he swore at the futility of the gesture. Somehow, these things must be stopped, but more important than that right now was the safety of these scores, these hundreds who fled through the bitter night from the path of death. It was more fearsome than any slaughter these poor victims could recognize, more awful than screaming gun shells or aerial bombs. Those at least were the fiendishness of men, but for this thing they saw no explanation at all.

The robots, if such they were, moved with the cold and silent efficiency of machines. They marched on and, now and again, two of their number would wheel from ranks to push down the front wall of a building. They were as systematic as a highly trained drill team. They towered enormous and the death they dealt was contemptuous. The overcast skies were releasing their pent clouds in torrential rain. The wet steel glistened as the massive arms swung, and still they marched on, and another tenement crashed; other scores fled screaming from their path— or screamed, trapped beneath the falling debris!

Nita called up to Wentworth urgently, "The police are on the way, Dick! I heard Kirkpatrick's voice. They're sending an emergency wagon, and reserves!"

Wentworth swore deeply. He jumped to the ground and snatched up the microphone that connected with the two-way radio of the car, swiftly sent out a call for Kirkpatrick.

"Wentworth calling Kirkpatrick," he snapped. "Wentworth calling Kirkpatrick…" He got his answer and rushed on. "Eight steel robots are wrecking tenements, killing people, Kirk," he said. "They are bullet-proof and even a car cannot knock them over. *Do not send your men against them. They will only be slaughtered!* Send for fire equipment! Send for Fifth Avenue buses. A charge by big trucks may knock them down! Nothing less will serve."

Even as he spoke, he heard the wail of sirens and Kirkpatrick's voice burst out from the receiver with a volume that meant the commissioner was very close. He was ordering his blue cohorts into battle!

Wentworth swore at Kirkpatrick's stubbornness, but there was a pallor in his cheeks at realization of what this meant. Kirkpatrick no longer even trusted him as an ally!

"But they'll be killed!" Nita cried. "Why is Stanley doing a thing like that?"

Wentworth shook his head. "That does not matter," he said quietly. "Take this car away from here, when I call to you. You may meet me later down Sutton Place."

"But, Dick, surely if the police...."

Wentworth had swung to the pavement. From the rear compartment, he removed the robes of the Spider and the steel mask which Nita had worn in lieu of make-up, which was a replica of the Spider's countenance.

"Go now," he said, "and there must be no disobedience!"

NITA NODDED, white-faced, and fought the car into a U-turn. Men clambered on the running board, scrambled upon its top to escape from the on-pressing terror from behind, and the coupé limped out of sight with a dozen fugitives clinging to it. A long spring hurled Wentworth into a dark doorway and, instants later, a somber and sinister figure crept out again into the shadows, a figure with hunched shoulders from which a long cape flowed; whose beetling brows were hidden beneath the low broad brim of a black hat. Any man who saw him now would recognize the Spider, but so great was the fear of these panic-driven people that they failed to see even the Master of Men!

Wentworth's eyes searched the facades of the tenements ahead of the robots. The people there already were aroused by the march of the steel monsters; the inhabitants already were fleeing. So much had been accomplished by the screams of the victims. The very air shivered now to the rhythms of the march of the steel men. Wentworth turned his back upon them and peered toward the shriek of the sirens. An instant later, the red-eyed limousine of the commissioner of police whipped into the street. On the instant, Wentworth was in action!

With the Spider's robes whipping out behind him, he hurled himself straight toward Kirkpatrick's car! Twin guns were in his fists and, as he raced forward, he began to shoot!

Two shots exploded the front tires of the police limousine. It yawed wildly, slewed to a halt, and the doors were batted open. A squad car whined around the corner in its wake, screamed to a halt, and police erupted from it also. Wentworth stood squarely in the middle of the street and the guns flamed in his hands—but the lead screamed high above the heads of the police!

For a long minute he stood there, a plain target for a score of guns, while he shouted defiance at the police. It was just the instant before police guns began to hammer at him that he leaped aside and fled toward the tenements that lined the way! It was a daring move, daringly executed, but the Spider was willing to risk his life endlessly to save these policemen. Lead made the air about him alive. He felt bullets tug at his whipping cape. His hat jarred upon his head, and then he dived into the shelter of a doorway. There was a smile on his lips. The police would follow him, and he would lead them a close chase, showing himself every now and then. By the time he had eluded them, the danger from the robots should be over....

Even as the thought crossed his mind, he heard Kirkpatrick's voice rasp out on the loudspeaker attached to his car for direction of his men in battle.

"Come back!" Kirkpatrick shouted. "Return to positions! The Spider is only a decoy for these men in steel. Their ally! Return to your posts!"

Something like a sob drove out between Wentworth's clenched teeth. Even his risking death had not served to save the police from the doom that would overtake them if they attacked the robots! He whirled about to face the police, but they had already obeyed Kirkpatrick's orders. They were returning to their posts—and to certain death!

Wentworth darted back toward the street, heard the volley fire of the police. They had swung the squad car broadside across the street in the path of the marching robots. Machine guns hammered from behind that barrier. A gas gun boomed deeply and the shell burst against the armor of the leading robot. The giant of steel did not even falter in its even, implacable stride!

Glaring toward those impregnable titans, Wentworth saw them perform the maneuver they had executed before. Two of them swung ponderously from line and marched to the front of a tenement building. They placed their hands against the front wall, and there was a dull rumbling explosion. As they pivoted back then toward the ranks, the tenement wall crumpled in upon itself. It was a feast of destruction, and the robots paid no more attention to the onslaught of the police than if the bullets had been a buzzing swarm of mosquitoes!

WENTWORTH SAW Kirkpatrick knuckle his mustache, then turn sharply toward Sergeant Reams at his side, as always. Reams ran toward the squad wagon and, a moment later, returned with a loose canvas bag that Wentworth knew contained hand grenades. With a final word to the police about him, ordering them to hold their positions, Kirkpatrick marched forward to meet the robots!

The sheer courage of that maneuver stopped Wentworth's breath in his lungs… but he did not wait to see the inevitable end of that reckless attack. Instead, he whirled and raced back through the hallways of the tenement, out into the street beyond. First Avenue was only a block away and there was a ceaseless parade of heavy trucks there. It was the only hope against these monsters. If he could seize a truck of sufficient mass….

Traffic stalled with screaming brakes when the awful figure of the Spider dashed out into the street, but Wentworth wove a rapid way through them toward the truck he had selected. It was a gigantic cement mixer, weighing more than ten tons. As he raced toward it, the driver slammed on his power brakes and leaped to the earth. He fled, screaming, toward the sidewalk. An instant later, Wentworth had hurled himself behind the wheel and had ground the accelerator to the floor. The great truck gathered speed slowly, then faster. Behind the wheel, Wentworth's face was set grimly. There was small protection for him here, but if he could save Kirkpatrick….

Wentworth manipulated the truck into the street where the robots marched. As the heavy machine straightened out, he heard the burst of a grenade and saw the white fury of its flame as it shattered between two of the robots. One of the steel giants staggered sideways a half-stride. Afterward, it stood motionless and slowly lifted a long, steel arm! Wentworth knew what that portended! The thing was getting ready to shoot Kirkpatrick!

Before flame spurted from the leveled forefinger of the monster, another grenade burst nearby. This time, the giant did not stagger, but apparently Kirkpatrick was unharmed, for two more grenades burst among the huddle of steel men! Then a great voice boomed out in the narrow street, a voice that had the rumbling accents of thunder! It was the first time Wentworth had heard one of the robots speak, and, strangely, the Spider smiled! For the voice that issued from one of those tanks-on-foot was human!

Wentworth had not realized until that moment how powerfully these impregnable giants had worked upon his imagination. Despite their horror, and their incredible strength; despite the futility of the attack he was about to launch, it was a relief to know that they were human beings under their shells!

But the robots were mustering in close ranks now that filled the street from side to side, and even as Wentworth approached them from behind… the robots began once more to march forward! The grenades that burst among them seemed no more than the echo of their steely tread. They did not even bother to shoot! What need, when the ponderous weight of their march, the swing of their derrick arms could crush out anyone who dared to impede their progress?

Wentworth's lips drew bitterly thin. He slipped the steel mask over his face, and wrung the last ounce of speed from the truck… and headed straight for the dose-marching ranks of the robots! YET, EVEN in his extremity, Wentworth did not drive blindly. He knew by now that the robots were almost impervious to blows. The impact of the truck would be less than the force of an exploding grenade. But he had a plan. The robots marched in two ranks of four men each. It was Wentworth's plan to part those ranks, to smash into the steel giants squarely between two of the men in the rear rank. If he had enough strength, he thought that he would drive those two men aside against their companions. He might even reach the front rank. After that....

Wentworth slammed the truck into second gear an instant before he reached the robots. One of the steel monsters turned its head, started a beam-like arm toward him... and was too late. With a crash like the collapse of a skyscraper, Wentworth drove the mighty truck squarely between the two middle robots! A grenade burst overhead at the same instant, and metal fragments punched down through the cab where Wentworth crouched. The impact of the collision hurled him violently against the wheel, but he kept his foot upon the accelerator, kept the truck grinding in second gear.

For an instant, Wentworth thought that even this attack had failed. Then the robot on his right was swung half-about and driven to its knees. Its upflung arms clashed against the giant on its right, and the steel fist rank like an anvil. The second robot reeled sideways, crashed against a tenement wall. The brick balustrade at the top of the wall tipped forward and rained down into the street. The fragments rang on the steel armor, but did not dent it. Two robots had partly fallen, and a third took long reeling strides forward, off-balance from the powerful impact of the ten-ton truck. But there were still five other robots which had not been disturbed by the charge. They were turning to confront Wentworth, with that ponderous slowness that was in itself fearfully ominous, bespeaking the power of those steel-thewed monsters. Wentworth thrust himself backward from the wheel, where the blow had thrown him. His breath had been driven from his body, and he was dizzy with shock. He saw one of the robots lift a slow, deadly finger to shoot him!

Wentworth slammed the gear into reverse and whipped out one of his heavy automatics. It was a futile thing in his hand, a popgun against artillery, but Wentworth flung up its muzzle with swift sureness. This was the gun that had saved his life in a thousand battles with the lords of the underworld, and he was a past master at its use. What he attempted would have balked many famous experts with firearms… but it was the Spider who held this gun!

One shot he fired, then the truck leaped backward under the surge of power he pumped into the engine. And the robot's hand suddenly spurted out a burst of flame! The right forefinger had exploded, for Wentworth had deftly plugged its muzzle with lead from his own swift gun!

The next moment, the truck had backed out of danger, and Wentworth had a moment's respite in which to plan his next move. He knew now that it was useless to charge the robots even with this mighty juggernaut. And next time, they would be ready; would meet him with a rain of bullets. He strained his eyes to see beyond the crowded ranks of the robots. Were the police retreating yet? Or was Kirkpatrick foolishly leading them to a new attack? He could not see—but he knew Kirkpatrick!

EVEN WHILE he cursed the stubbornness of Kirkpatrick that would fling him again and again into this vain battle, Wentworth knew a grim admiration for the man. It was this very quality of perseverance that made him the most effective police commissioner the city had ever known! But he was beaten in advance this time. He and his brave men would only walk to their deaths!

With the thought, Wentworth knew what he must do, and he was already in action as the idea flashed across his mind. He backed the truck into the cross street, sent it lurching forward. A few minutes of maneuvering and then, gathering momentum, he headed straight for the tottering wall of a half-collapsed tenement that towered above the close-packed robots!

He knew that the wall would not destroy, or even stop the robots, but it would slow them for a few moments. It would give the Spider time enough to complete his work!

Grimly, Wentworth clung to the truck to the last possible moment, then he leaped from the running board, sprawled into the street. He bounded to his feet, and sprinted back the way he had come, but he had not taken a dozen strides when the truck slammed its tons of weight against the rocking tenement wall. There was an instant when a few bricks rained down on the battered steel truck, then a groaning crack opened up the face of the wall. It leaned gently forward. It bowed gracefully above the truck—then it lost its balance! Faster and faster, the solid wall of the tenement pitched forward. As it fell, many jagged cracks ran across its face. A window frame was popped out and sailed like a box kite ahead of the fall. That window frame smashed down over the head of a robot, and then the wave of bricks broke over the upright monsters of steel. Fragments flew upward as from an explosion, and the dust roiled high against the sleet-spitting sky. The concussion of the fall rolled thunder through the deserted streets.

But Wentworth took no notice of the collapse. Already he was circling toward where Kirkpatrick and his cohorts laid siege to the steel killers. They were rolled back by that wave of masonry. Kirkpatrick and Reams, their grenades exhausted, had quickly retreated before that impact. Wentworth saw this as he popped out of the doorway of a tenement which he had reached through the back court. He was within a dozen yards of Kirkpatrick's limousine, and like a black shadow, he slipped soundlessly across the street. There were a score of police within gunshot of him, but all stared where the dust of the building collapse still lifted a monstrous dark silhouette against the sky. Already, within that moiling cloud, there was movement. Wentworth saw a single robot lift an arm, then a leg... and thrust out of the edge of the wreckage!

A shivered, concerted moan went up from the men in police blue. They were brave, these men, but they could not fight immortals! Wentworth was squarely beside Kirkpatrick's car now. He straightened, and the driver twisted about, his face bewildered. Wentworth's hand darted like a snake's head, and his stiffened fingers drove to nerve centers in the man's throat, spilled him unconscious across the seat. It was the work of a moment to dump the man into the back, to pull on his uniform cap. Wentworth's lips were grim as he reached for the microphone of the loudspeaker unit, but when he spoke it was crisply, in the metallic tones which Kirkpatrick used!

"Retreat, men," he said, imitating Kirkpatrick. "We have done all we can. Return to quarters and await further orders. And make it fast! These monsters in steel are after us again!"

WENTWORTH SAW Kirkpatrick leap from the shadows where he had crouched to ambush the stirring giants, but the men behind the squad wagon did not suspect. They had heard Kirkpatrick's voice, they thought, and it was an order they welcomed. Within brief seconds, while Kirkpatrick raced toward his parked car, the squad car got under way. Then Kirkpatrick reached the running board, whipped open the door on the far side from Wentworth.

"Who the devil gave that order?" he demanded harshly. "Damn it, Cassidy...."

He did not notice until then that the man in the uniform cap wore a long black cape on his shoulders, or that the face that peered toward him through the gloom was the face of the Spider! When he did notice, Wentworth's fingers were already striking for his throat! Instantly the Spider hauled Kirkpatrick into the car. When Sergeant Reams bolted alongside the limousine, he looked into the muzzle of Wentworth's automatic!

"Get behind the wheel, Sergeant Reams," Wentworth ordered coldly, "and drive this, car away from here. Never mind the blown-out tires. The robots can't move rapidly enough to catch you!"

Reams' jaw set stubbornly, but the gray-blue eyes that glared at him through the steel mask were relentless; behind them blazed the will of the Spider. Reams muttered an oath, and took the wheel. As the car wheeled away, with Wentworth on the running board, he cast a single backward glance—and relief flooded through him!

The robots had had enough of the battle, and they were moving off toward the river as they hauled themselves out of the debris which Wentworth had dumped upon them. Wentworth's teeth were clenched together, and there was a coldness in his soul that was fury. God alone knew how many poor mortals had died this night under the march of the robots. But, God being willing, he would track the monsters to their lair beneath the waters of the East River!

"Straight on!" he ordered Reams harshly. "And if you love Kirkpatrick, don't revive him until it's too late to fight those robots! They're in full retreat... and it would only mean his death!"

As he finished, Wentworth dropped from the running board of the limousine and ducked into the shadows of a dark doorway. For a moment, he stood there watching the limousine jounce on its flat tires down the street. His lips were a little twisted. Kirkpatrick could be so true a friend—and so harsh an enemy! Too bad that they could not work side by side against crime, but Kirkpatrick was first of all a defender of the law. And it was because the law so often failed that the Spider had been born! WITH A jerk of his head, Wentworth bounded from the doorway and raced through the shadows. A half dozen blocks away, he ducked into the dead-end street where he had told Ram Singh to meet him; where Nita would be waiting. They called to him softly from a gap in the wall that surrounded the ruins of what had been once his fortress home—and which criminals had destroyed in one awful hour. Wentworth swerved toward the gateway, already stripping off the black cape about his shoulders.

"Quickly," he ordered, "get the diving suit ready!"

He saw Nita then, huddled against the broken wall for protection from the bite of the sleet. The Long Island shore was obscured and the black waters made a mournful obligate to the wind. A tug howled from the obscurity. Nita came toward him.

"Must you go… tonight, Dick?" she asked softly. "It will be terribly cold under the river."

Wentworth laughed harshly. "The robots are marching toward the river now," he said. "When they enter, I must follow!" He could see how white and drawn her face was, could see how she tried to smile as he stepped into the tight fitting rubber suit, and Ram Singh hurriedly made the fastenings secure.

"But, Dick… you'll be helpless under water! Those great murderous things will know you're following them."

Wentworth shook his head. "Perhaps," he said softly, "but under water, I will have a weapon against them! There are men inside those suits, Nita, and I will carry a knife!"

Nita stared at him incredulously. "A knife against bullet-proof armor!"

Wentworth laughed grimly. "It is the one weapon that can win! Hurry, Ram Singh, hurry. They will be here soon!"

Ram Singh prepared to hoist the heavy-copper diving helmet high, and Wentworth rapidly adjusted the oxygen valves. But Nita was standing very close, and he saw her shoulders shiver a little. Brave Nita… afraid. Wentworth laid his hand upon her arm, and then his head lifted. Stiffness ran through all his body, a stiffness that was the eagerness for battle.

The air was vibrating dully to that funereal rhythm he knew. He felt the earth quiver under the remorseless tread of the steel robots, and for an instant he looked dubiously at the long blade of the knife which would be his only weapon beneath the black waters of the East River. Then he laughed, harshly.

"Lock on the helmet, Ram Singh!" he ordered. "The hour of battle is here!"

CHAPTER 6
UNDER THE RIVER

THE BLACK waters of the East River heaved sullenly, dimpled by the slash of sleet. The thunderous tread of the robots was very close and, in the ruins of what had been his home, Wentworth crouched against the wall and drew Nita close to protect her. Ram Singh growled in his throat, his big hand close to his dagger.

Past the concealing shadows went the robots, whose marching feet had become an intolerable weight upon the brain, upon the heart. Only when they were past did Wentworth release Nita.

"Keep watch, if you like," Wentworth told her gently. "I'll be back within the hour. I won't follow too closely, but if I can track those robots to their hideout, I'll contrive a way to smash this whole damnable murder conspiracy!"

He pivoted then and moved heavily in the wake of the robots. They were already entering the water, one by one. The black waters lapped against their steel flanks, then closed quietly above those rounded helmets. Wentworth moved as heavily as a robot. There were leaden weights fastened to the belt that held the knife, and in his hands he had other leaden weights which could be fastened to his feet. He would need them beneath the surface of the river, but on land they made walking too difficult. When the last robot had disappeared, Wentworth broke into a lumbering run. At the water's edge, he paused to tighten the window in the front of his helmet, to slip his feet into the straps of the shoe weights. He touched the hilt of the knife at his belt, and his lips locked grimly. He floundered into the water.

The shore was slippery with mud and the river closed about his ankles. The water deepened instantly and within four strides, he was up to his neck. The weights were less hampering now. He was beginning to feel the buoyancy of his suit—and the cold of the water struck through the rubberized material. There had been no time to don heavy garments beneath it. No matter… He would not be below the surface long. Within a few minutes, he should know the lair of these monsters of steel, or be defeated. His gray-blue eyes narrowed, he rapidly checked the valves of his helmet—and took a final step.

The water lapped against the window in the helmet. For a moment the slap of the waves against the metal casque was thunderous… and then it stopped and he knew he was wholly beneath the water. The blackness was impenetrable. He groped across the chest of the suit, touched a hard spot in the rubber, and a powerful beam reached out from a glass port. Its range was only a few feet, but it lighted the ground at his feet. He was already ankle-deep in the sludge of the bottom. Perhaps he carried too much weight. He could tell better when he was deeper in the river. But now his eyes focused on the mud, and a thin smile twisted his lips. As he had expected, the huge steel feet of the robots had left their trail! It looked as if a herd of elephants had waded through soft mud. But those footmarks were even larger!

Wentworth bent against the thrust of the tide and dragged his weighted feet steadily forward. He had forgotten the bitter cold that was seeping

Wentworth knew now that he was trapped.

into his tight suit; forgotten everything save the chase. It was the first moment in all this mad night of battle that he had been able to put his mind entirely upon the problem of the robots. Mechanized monsters they undoubtedly were, but he was equally certain that they carried men inside them—and men as ruthless as if they were soulless robots! In heaven's name, who could be the leader, the director of this mad jihad of slaughter? But he had a clue to that, even though it was a lead he could not understand.

THREE RICH houses had been looted, smashed by the robots—and a fourth house just beside them, richer than the others, had not been looted. That fourth home had been guarded by a man of the Drexler agency, and on his chest was tattooed the sign of the murder monsters! Wentworth had always had the highest regard for Frank Drexler, and he was loath even now to believe the man capable of such infamies. And yet... there was the evidence of the Drexler guard, and the trail of the robots led upstream toward Drexler's riverside home!

Now that he was farther from the shore, the force of the current was extremely powerful. It was labor to set each foot before the other; labor too to drag his weighted legs free of the sucking mud upon the river bottom. Swirls of it lifted like torpid dust to cloud against the shortened ray of his lamp. There was numbness in his limbs that was the creeping paralysis of cold. Wentworth was like that, canted forward at a forty-five-degree angle against the current, fighting for each step, when the light reached out and wrapped itself about him.

For an instant Wentworth thought that it was the blinding

reflection of his own lamp, hurled back by the higher swirl of the mud. Then he realized that the light was far more powerful than his own. A muffled oath burst from his lips and crashed deafeningly within the helmet. He twisted his head about, peered out of the small side port in the helmet—and then his hand flicked to the knife at his waist! Peering at him from the black wall of the water were two great balls of light and he realized as he stared at them, that the light poured from the eyes of one of the robots! God, he had been a fool! He should have guessed that they would post a rear guard!

Wentworth ripped the knife from its sheath, but he had no intention of battling the robot in these depths if he could avoid it. His purpose was to find their lair, and then to arrange for its destruction. He wrenched his feet free of the mud, tried to thrust himself swiftly upstream. He moved with incredible speed for a diver, but it was slow, terribly slow. The robot moved with the same implacable pace that it used upon land, neither faster nor slower. It was too powerful to heed either mud or water pressure. The glare of the lights glittered from the steel. The knees lifted steadily, the feet swung forward six feet at a stride!

After that single instant of struggle, Wentworth realized that flight was useless. If he was to go on with his pursuit—and it was characteristic of the Spider's indomitable purpose that he did not even consider abandoning his task!—there was only one possible course. He must destroy this robot!

On the face of it, the thought was madness. Bullets and the head-long charge of trucks had not stopped these monsters, nor had the impact of a wall of brick done more than delay them for

89

a space of moments! Yet, with only that slim-bladed knife which he gripped in a cold-numbed hand, Wentworth turned to face the enemy! His mouth was a lipless gash across his face, and his eyes were narrowed and intent. He shifted his feet in the silt of the bottom, kicked free of their weights. His left hand moved rapidly upon the weights that were attached to his belt. There were five of them, weighing ten pounds each.

The robot was only two strides away now and Wentworth swiftly unfastened three of the five weights from his belt. The buoyancy of his suit immediately made itself felt. His feet felt light. Wentworth poised the knife before him like a sword and, with a tensing of his leg muscles, he dived straight at the robot! The current plucked him up and hurled him forward. The light from the robot's eyes was suddenly dazzling, but in its reflection Wentworth could make out the great steel body. He saw then that the two massive beams of the arms were swinging forward, and that the steel talons were clenched to seize him! Once let those points rake his rubber suit, and they would tear it to shreds!

BUT WENTWORTH had no intention of being caught. With less weight he had gained considerable swiftness of movement. As the right arm of the steel monster swung toward him, Wentworth jack-knifed and swept in under it. It was the moment for which he had waited. His knife point rasped across the steel armor until it found the armpit. As he had discovered when he hurled bullets at the monster, the joints of the armor were covered by overhangs of steel… but there were joints, and in order to keep out the water, *they must be covered by rubber!*

It was this deduction on which Wentworth had gambled his life. Now, probing deeply into the socket of the armor, he felt the knife catch on some soft, half-yielding substance and exultation coursed hotly through his veins. It did not matter whether this was a mechanical monster, or whether a human being was within it, if water trickled inside, it spelled the robot's doom!

Wentworth seized the shoulder of the robot with his left hand, and thrust more deeply with his probing steel. He knew that the robot was in violent motion, for the water swirled fiercely about him, but he clung tightly, fought to widen the slit he had made in the rubber. He thought that, already, the motions of the robot had become slower. A few more moments of clinging to this creature's back, where it could not reach him, and he would have the robot disabled. Afterward, he could press on with his pursuit, and then....

A cry surged to Wentworth's lips. He had thought the robot could not reach him, but he had been wrong! Even in his moment of triumph, he felt a steel hand close like a vise about his ankle! It pulled at him resistlessly, and Wentworth's hold was instantly torn loose. He had just time to wrench his knife free when he was whirled in a frenzied circle through the waters! His arms flung wide, and centrifugal force drove the blood to his brain so that his senses faded. Presently, he realized that the motion had ceased; that he was being held aloft before the dazzling lights that were the eyes of the robot. But it was only for an instant, and then there was a tremendous pressure upon his helmet; blood started from his nostrils. He heard the thin creaking of strained metal and horror shot through him like the punch of a bullet. God in heaven, the robot *was crushing Wentworth's helmet!*

Even as the thought slashed through Wentworth's brain, the first jet of water struck Wentworth's cheek with the shock of a blow. It was fiercely cold, and the weight of the river drove it inward with terrific force. Then another jet… The robot was deliberately delaying the moment when he would drown Wentworth, torturing him! Fury swirled through Wentworth's brain. Once more he struck out with the knife, and this time it found a joint near the throat of the steel monster. Savagely, Wentworth thrust the knife home, dragged its keen edge through the rubber inner shield.

There was a single convulsive drag at Wentworth's leg, and then his helmet was ripped from his head. The river crowded into his nostrils, beat in upon his eardrums, hammered its intolerable pressure upon every exposed inch of his body. His lungs were bursting; he was being squeezed to death, and still the steel talons of the robot gripped his ankle.

Then suddenly, Wentworth was in darkness. For a dizzy moment, he thought that his senses were blotted out and then, dimly, exultation crept through him. He knew then that the robot's lights were out, and he knew the reason… water had reached the mechanism of the robot! Dear God, suppose he had jammed the mechanism so that his foot could not be released? He—there was a swirl of water about him, and Wentworth felt himself dragged more deeply toward the river's bottom. The robot had fallen!

HOW MANY seconds had passed? How many more

moments of consciousness remained? Wentworth could not estimate. He only knew that death was close. The coldness was already having its paralyzing way with him. He thought of his knife, and an idea drove itself into his fading mind. He began to hack at the rubber suit, to slit the leg of the diving outfit which was gripped in the robot's hand.

How he accomplished that thing, Wentworth could not guess. He only knew that he was shooting upward toward the surface, toward open air. His lungs were aching, and there was a heavy pounding in his temples, in his ears. He must breathe *now*. He must! His head broke the surface of the river!

Somehow, Wentworth managed to keep himself afloat, but when a hand clamped upon his arm, there was in him no will to fight. The cold had eaten into his bones. Presently, he knew that it was his powerful Sikh bodyguard, Ram Singh, who had plunged into the flood to save him… There were moments when the whole universe whirled dizzily about his head, yet an urgency goaded him. There was a task he must perform, a task… if he could remember….

At last he knew that Nita and Ram Singh were beside him, that they were hurrying him toward the car. The warmth of the heated interior swirled against his skin, yet did not seem to penetrate. He began to shiver, and he found that he could think… and remember.

"Northward," he ordered Ram Singh sharply. "Go to the Drexler home."

"No, Dick!" Nita cried. "Even you can't stand exposure like that!"

Wentworth shook his head and crouched toward the heater. There was a gauntness about his drawn face, and fierce fires in his eyes. "There is no time," he said hoarsely. "The robots are marching upriver. If I am right, and they are going to the Drexler home, my only chance is to be there when they arrive. No, Nita, I can't stop to get on dry clothing."

Nita said no more, but her lips tightened. She handed him a flask of brandy, and Wentworth tipped it to his lips. Its warmth was grateful, but it did not send the familiar tingle through his veins. Exposure, after the exhaustion of the night, had been severe. Nita was right of course… He shook his head. There was no time. His eyes stared piercingly ahead through the half-moons the windshield wipers cut in the sleet. It was in the cellar of the Drexler home that he must look for the entrance of the robots….

"As soon as I leave you," Wentworth said slowly, "you will find a taxi and go home, Nita. I must wear the robes of the Spider. Ram Singh will wait and rush me home afterward. And I'll get on something dry then."

Nita leaned close to him, "Dick, you mean that you will not be through then? There is still more to be done?"

Wentworth's blue lips smiled. Was it any new thing that the Spider's work was never done?

"There is one more job tonight," he said slowly, "if I fail at Drexler's… I killed a robot on the bottom of the river. I must get another diving suit and arrange to recover that robot. Once we have learned the secret of the Iron Man, we can beat him!"

Nita caught hold of Wentworth's shoulder, forced him to

look at her. "Dick, you can't do it," she said. "Let Ram Singh dive for you."

Wentworth laughed, but it was tenderly… and a sharp, painful cough broke his laughter. His jaw set stubbornly. "When I have finished, I will rest," he said. "Ram Singh, turn right at the next corner. Pull into a doorway of that warehouse and stop! Nita, there is a taxi stand around the corner."

WITHOUT A word, Nita climbed from the car. She reached up to clasp his face between her hands and kiss him, and then she half-ran, half-stumbled toward the corner. Her head was down… Wentworth watched her for a moment, and shivered. There was a weakness in his chest and the cold refused to leave his limbs. He swore at his own softness, donned the robes of the Spider.

Beside him, Ram Singh said eagerly, "Orders, *sahib?*"

Wentworth shook his head. "Stay in the car, Ram Singh," he said, "and watch. If I signal you…."

Disappointment clouded the Sikh's eyes, but he salaamed his acknowledgment. Wentworth slipped away into the shadows. The wind prodded beneath the cape, but Wentworth forgot the cold as he peered toward the Drexler house. It was a survival of Manhattan's early days. Once a farmhouse on a point that jutted out into the river, it was walled in now by factories and warehouses, dwarfed by a modern apartment building. But, due to its location, it still maintained isolation. And it was very close to the river banks! That fact was important!

Only dim lights were burning behind the small old-fashioned windows of the house. Wentworth was a shadow that drifted across the street, sliding over the wall. A window on the second floor was open and, in brief moments, Wentworth had climbed to it.

Presently, the Spider mingled with the darkness in the room. There was a bed against the wall in which a man slept. Doubtfully, Wentworth drifted toward it. If Drexler were at home, in bed… A faint radiance was all that showed when Wentworth squeezed a masked flashlight. Its pallid light crept across the bed, fell on a frail, wrinkled hand that was almost transparent with age; stole up until it illumined the head upon the pillow. Straggling white hair, a ruff of whiskers, a lined and sunken face. This must be old Angus Drexler, Wentworth decided. He would have to be careful. The aged slept so lightly.…

Rapidly then, Wentworth canvassed the upper floor of the house, found the servant's room where a maid slept, but no trace of Frank Drexler! Wentworth's lips clamped together thinly then as he stole down the narrow, winding steps. It might mean nothing at all that Drexler was out on this bitter night when the robots marched. Still, Drexler's home was an ideal base for the robots. There were two possibilities of a hideout: One beneath the garage, the other under the house itself. An underwater entrance, perhaps.…

The warmth of the basement flooded up to meet Wentworth. He heard the whirring of an oil burner and his light reached out to quest over the stone walls, centered abruptly on a steel door that opened on the side toward the river! In a half dozen quick strides, Wentworth was before the door.

THE LOCK yielded under Wentworth's skillful fingers and

he listened a moment before he eased it open. Darkness beyond, and the musty rich odors of… wine! Once more, Wentworth's flashlight licked out. Stairs led downward into a wine cellar. Its stone walls were lined with bottle bins and hogsheads. Across the ceiling ran asbestos-wrapped steam pipes, and Wentworth's eyes followed them intently. They turned into an alcove on the left-hand wall!

Wentworth flicked on the lights and with long bounds crossed the cellar. The pipes burrowed through the stone wall into the solid earth beyond! Narrow-eyed, he studied those pipes. They ran in the direction of the garage. Was that their sole purpose?

Instantly, Wentworth was at work on the stone wall, seeking some hidden doorway. He frowned as he tried to make swift calculations of time. Could the robots yet have reached a secret hiding place here? Impossible to estimate the time spent beneath the surface of the river, but it could not have been very long. Probably the robots would be just arriving, if this were their destination. Wentworth swore softly. He could detect no signs of an opening in the walls, no trace of footsteps upon the earthen floor. The hogsheads… Wentworth approached them. They were backed against the stone wall through which the pipes pierced. In an instant, he was at the spigots. If any of these proved… *empty!*

But wine flowed briefly from each spigot. Aroma was sharp in his nostrils. Nothing here. Nothing that he could detect. There remained the garage, but he must be swift, swift. At any moment, Drexler might appear—or the robots.

"Up with your hands, Spider!" a voice commanded harshly. "What the hell are doing here?"

Wentworth swore softly. He recognized the voice at once— Frank Drexler! Even in the face of that discovery, had he been sure of the man's guilt, he could have drawn his gun and fired, with a fair chance of escaping. But the Spider did not war against innocent men, not even suspected men. He had to be very sure! So the Spider's hands went up slowly, and he turned to peer up into the face of Frank Drexler!

The detective was fully twenty feet away, crouched at the head of the wooden steps that descended into the wine cellar. Pale fire glowed suddenly in the Spider's gray-blue eyes. *For Drexler's clothing was dripping wet!*

"Speak up!" Drexler ordered sharply. "What are you doing here?"

The Spider's disguised face moved in a smile that was full of mocking menace. "I had heard," he said softly, "that you possessed a very fine cellar. But I had expected to find your wines in steel casks."

Anger flushed Drexler's cheek, and Wentworth was aware of movement behind the man; saw the old, peering face of Drexler's father.

"The Spider, hey?" old Drexler's voice was thin, rasping. "What are you waiting for, son? Burn the man down!"

Drexler jerked his head. "Go call the police, father," he said. "He won't get away from me.

THE WRINKLED face blinked down at Wentworth. Aged

hands trembled on the head of the cane on which he leaned. Old Drexler's eyes were as excited as a boy's.

"Are you sure," Wentworth asked softly, "that you want the police here, Drexler? You will gain considerable publicity by capturing the Spider, but you're already a rather prosperous man, Drexler. You are rapidly becoming more so, aren't you?"

Drexler said savagely, "I want an answer to my question, and a direct one. What the hell are you doing here?"

"I was beginning to tell you, Drexler," Wentworth said sharply. "Keep your mouth shut, and listen!"

The old man lifted the knotted cane and shook it, "Don't you talk to Frank like that!" he cried. "Burn him down, Frank!"

Neither of the two men paid any heed to him. Wentworth was close to the wine bins. It would take only a flick of the wrist to seize a bottle and smack out the single overhead light... but Drexler's gun rested on him unwaveringly. Yet Wentworth thought that he saw a way. The father seemed senile, and child-like in his adoration of Frank Drexler. If he could infuriate the old man to the point where he attempted to interfere....

Wentworth said, "Three houses were robbed on Sutton Place tonight, just beside one guarded by your agency. *But the house your man watched was untouched!* That man had on his chest the symbol of a criminal who has killed dozens of human beings this night!"

The old man said, quaveringly, "He's calling you a crook, Frank!"

Wentworth nodded. "That's right! I'm calling you a thief who betrays his own clients, Drexler! I'm calling you a murderer!"

99

Drexler was unmoved, but the old man lifted the gnarled stick in his hand and shook it violently. "Why, damn you!" he cried shrilly. "You can't talk to Frank like that! Give me that gun, Frank! Give me—"

Drexler's face twitched with concern. "Be quiet, father!" he said sharply. "Remember your heart! Look out—"

As Drexler spoke, the old man pushed past him indignantly. Drexler's head whipped toward him… and Wentworth struck! He seized a wine bottle, flung it, and there was the sharp explosion as the light went out. Drexler's gun thundered, but the Spider already was in motion!

He vaulted atop the hogsheads and he ran lightly across them while Drexler's gun thundered again. Through the explosions, Wentworth caught another menacing sound. Somewhere above, a bell was pealing violently—a burglar alarm! Then there was the tramp of rushing feet! It was either the police, or more men of the Drexler agency, and either way it meant deadly peril to the Spider!

The thought lent fury to Wentworth's speed. Two more leaps put him beside the open-work of the stairs. He could hear Drexler's hoarse whisper as he urged his father to retreat. Wentworth waited for no more. His hand flashed out and closed on Drexler's ankle! A wrench sent the man stumbling wildly down the steps, and the Spider was racing across the windowless basement toward its only exit. The tramp of feet overhead was thunderous now. Long bounds took Wentworth up the steps… too late. As he reached them, the door at their head was wrenched open. An instant later, brilliant lights poured downward… and found only the empty cellar, the steel door across its width swinging open, and an old man there who waved a knotted cane violently! SERGEANT REAMS clattered fiercely down the steps, followed an instant later by Kirkpatrick. The commissioner's voice rang out crisply, "Kelly, take the head of the steps. Let no one out!"

Then Kirkpatrick, followed by two more uniformed men, was striding across the basement. Drexler's flushed angry face showed in the entrance of the wine room.

"There was shooting here!" Kirkpatrick snapped. "What was it?"

Drexler was tight-lipped. "Maybe I was having some target-practice," he snapped. "Who gave you permission to enter here?"

"Gun-fire gives any police officer the right to enter," Kirkpatrick said grimly. "Otherwise, we would have waited for you to answer the door. And you haven't answered my question yet, Drexler. I have a number to ask you about tonight's happenings!"

The two men glared at each other, and suddenly a voice rang through the basement. It seemed to be the voice of Kirkpatrick, and it was imperative.

"Kelly!" it ordered. "Down here! Quick!"

The guard at the head of the steps came down instantly. Kirkpatrick swore and whirled toward him.

Drexler's voice lifted, clearly. "It's the Spider! I thought he'd got clear!"

In that moment of confusion, a black figure darted from beneath the stairs. Before Kelly sensed a mistake, strong arms clasped him from behind. He was lifted off his feet, dragged backwards up the stairs. Sergeant Reams' gun was in his fist. Kirkpatrick whipped out his long-barreled revolver and raced across the cellar so that he could command a side shot at the steps... and they were all too late. Despite the struggles of the surprised Kelly, Wentworth had reached the head of the stairs!

For an instant, he paused there. Then Kelly reeled down the steps, the door clapped shut, and from behind it the mocking laughter of the Spider sounded. It died in a burst of savage gunfire as the police sent their lead screaming toward that flimsy door.

But Wentworth already had reached a side window of the house. He peered out long enough to spot the guards at the gate and, once more, he called out in the urgent tones of Kirkpatrick.

"In here, fast!" he called. "We've got the Spider trapped!"

There were sharp shouts and the men dashed for the front door of the house. In an instant Wentworth was out the window and racing toward the wall. He staggered as he dropped to the street beyond, raced for the side street in which he had left the car. Even as he ran, he heard the shouts of his pursuers burst out more loudly, and knew that his subterfuge had been discovered. He reeled a little as he ran, and there was a sharp pain in his side. God, he could not afford illness now! He could not even afford rest....

The robots must have landed, already; or the gunfire had kept them in hiding—or they had never headed for the Drexler place at all! The Spider must return to the river with a fresh diving suit and reclaim that fallen robot.

A SHUDDER raced through him at the thought of those frigid depths. He staggered more violently, and then the coupé spurted from the mouth of the dark street, skidded to a momentary halt beside him and raced on as he sprang to the running board. He opened the door, dropped inside. Ram Singh was bent grimly over the wheel, and Nita was smiling up at him. She was holding a steaming thermos of coffee in her hand. "It's been laced with brandy, Dick," she said quietly. "Drink it!"

Wentworth looked backward. Already, Kirkpatrick's limousine was lunging forward. Its siren began to wail. Wentworth's lips drew thinly.

"You've put yourself in deadly danger, Nita," he said quietly, "just to make me drink a little coffee!"

Nita smiled faintly, "It's my right, isn't it Dick?" she asked quietly. "I have so few… Drink up, Dick!"

Wentworth's lips clamped grimly together, but he made no other answer as he reached for the coffee. Nita needed no other. She closed her eyes as Wentworth lifted the thermos bottle to his lips. Her hands clenched whitely in her lap. Wentworth shuddered and gasped at the drink.

"I know," Nita said hurriedly. "It's awful stuff, but the best I could find in the neighborhood. You should choose your parking places more carefully, Dick!"

Wentworth tilted the bottle again. There was a pain in his chest. It wouldn't help the battle any if he came down with pleurisy! Nonsense. Another hour now, and he could rest. A brief expedition beneath the river to fasten cables to that robot, and then… He lifted a hand uncertainly to his forehead.

"This heat is making me a little sleepy," he said slowly.

Nita whispered, "If you would only rest a little while, Dick! Ram Singh and I can handle this robot."

Wentworth shook his head. "Has there been any word of Jackson?" he asked heavily.

Nita said, "None!"

Ram Singh looked toward her swiftly, but she shook her head and he did not speak. She was watching Wentworth closely. His whole body was relaxing. Her hand trembled as she slid her arm about his shoulders.

Wentworth shook himself, "Nita!" he said clearly. "Nita, you've drugged me!"

Nita's lips twisted with her smile. "Yes, lover," she whispered. "I promise your work will go on, but you must sleep! You must, Dick! I only hope it isn't too late to save you from pneumonia!"

Wentworth tried to fight off the heaviness that was in his brain and he could not. His head sank toward Nita's shoulder. Behind them, the sirens yelped with the vicious insistence of the chase. The powerful motor under the coupé's battered hood made the whole car tremble. But Nita heeded none of these things. Her face was very grave as she stared straight before her. She had taken a fearful responsibility upon herself; none knew that better than she. They were still in genuine danger from the police, and Dick was unconscious from the drugs. She depended on Ram Singh to take them to safety, but that was only the beginning. There was a task for the Spider still to be performed. SWIFTLY, NITA began to remove the garb of the Spider in which Wentworth still was wrapped. With tender hands, she stripped off the disguise which turned his rugged, kindly face into the ominous mask of the Spider.

"This had to be done, Ram Singh," she said heavily, and she knew that she spoke more to reassure herself than to explain to the Sikh. "Otherwise, there wasn't a chance that he would escape pneumonia. And it would not help for him to know now about Jackson. It should be simple enough to clear Jackson now that everyone knows about the robots. It was a brave thing he did in trying to get rid of that policeman's body, even though it did end in arrest and a charge of murder!"

Ram Singh murmured, *"Han, missie sahib!"* His tone held no conviction.

Nita's jaw set solidly. There were doubts in Ram Singh's mind, too, but she would prove she was right!

"Shake off these police!" she ordered, and a sharpness of command crept into her voice that made it strangely resemble Wentworth's. "And hurry! We have so little time until dawn!"

Ram Singh said nothing, but his head lifted more alertly. He had never taken orders from any other woman. It would have been beneath his dignity as a lion, a Singh among Sikhs. But when that tone crept into the voice of the *missie sahib,* he knew that it was the mate of the *sahib* who spoke! *Wah,* no evil could come to the master through her! Was not her *karma* one with his?

Nita, watching him, nodded her head slowly as she saw the change. "There will be fighting ahead, warrior of the Sikhs!" she said softly, in the Punjabi Wentworth had taught her. "There will be a vengeance for thy knife!"

Ram Singh's laughter rumbled. *"Wah*, thy warrior is ready, *missie sahib!"* he cried. "Already, the jackals of the police lose our trail!"

Ram Singh was right. Fifteen minutes later the coupé slid to a halt on the street beside Wentworth's apartment house. Ram Singh carried Wentworth's body, tenderly as a child's, in his arms and they sped upward in the private elevator. Swiftly then, Nita aroused the aged butler, old Jenkyns who had served Wentworth's father before him. Into his hands, gentle as a woman, she gave the man she loved… and then swung to face Ram Singh.

"Another diving suit, Ram Singh," she said quietly. "We will need the *sahib's* Diesel-powered cruiser."

The Sikh bowed in a low salaam. *Wah*, here was a woman a brave man could follow! She would do the master's work while he slept; Ram Singh hummed through his nose, a war song of his native hills, as he hurried about the tasks Nita had set him. Nita smiled faintly at the change in the Sikh, and then she bent gently over the sleeping Wentworth.

"Have the doctor in at once, Jenkyns," she said. "Tell him, I gave Master Richie codeine. When he wakes, I should be here. If I am not…" Nita straightened and her eyes lifted to the wrinkled, kindly eyes of Jenkyns. Her voice grew crisper. "If I am not, you will tell him that I went after the robot at the bottom of the river."

Jenkyns' eyes were worried, "You shouldn't, Miss Nita," he said gently. "The master will worry—"

Nita smiled, "Please, Jenkyns. Give him my message."

SHE STRODE from the room and Ram Singh hurried

down the hall with the equipment she had ordered. It was a heavy burden even for his stalwart shoulders, and Nita's own back straightened in anticipation of the load she must carry, both physical and mental. Her head was up as she followed Ram Singh down the corridor and into the elevator. At least Dick was taken care of….

Nita sat quietly in the cabin of the Diesel cruiser as Ram Singh drove it slowly up the East River. The tide was slack at extreme ebb, and that would help a little. But she would have to do her work before it turned. She looked down at herself, encased in the thick rubber diving suit with the leaden weights at her slim waist. The helmet rested beside her on the seat. She was ready. Her lips moved in a slight smile. Ram Singh would be her only help. He had been ferociously eager to make the descent, but she could not allow it. She had taken the responsibility for placing Dick out of the battle. She could not permit anyone else to carry on in his stead.

Overhead, the storm whined and blustered. The cold was intense, but at least the overcast sky would delay the light of dawn. She would need the time… Ram Singh's heel thudded twice on the deck. It was the signal!

Nita pushed herself to her feet, picked up the helmet and bore it before her in both arms. The weights were on deck. Ram Singh would attach them at the last moment before lowering her over the side. Nita thrust out into the night, heard the motors check and the rush of the anchor rope. Then she was clear of the cabin's protection and the storm was upon her. The sleet laid jewels upon her clustering curls, and Ram Singh moved with swift efficiency. He lifted the helmet over her head, spun the anchoring bolts fast.

"Any orders, *missie sahib?*" Ram Singh asked.

Nita shook her head. "Haul up if I yank the line three times," she said quietly. "Use the winch if I pull twice. That's all!"

Nita's hand rested on the knife hilt at her waist, but she knew it would be feeble in her hands. She had a gun beneath the rubber suit, and she did not even tell herself why she carried it there. She smiled into Ram Singh's anxious eyes.

"Don't worry, Ram Singh," she said quietly. "You know I've made these dives before. Help me over the side!"

The black waters seemed eager for her. She made an adjustment of the oxygen inlet, of the exhaust valve, took a few steps down the ladder. Then she swung off into the water.

Nita felt the vibration of the rope, slipping out slowly through Ram Singh's hands, felt the pull of the current. No light at all reached her here, but she needed none as yet Ram Singh knew the spot at which he had rescued Dick, and the robot could not be far from there. If there were other robots here, she would not see them until they had come too close for her to escape!

Nita closed her eyes and tried to hold the smile on her lips. Dick, at least, was safe. She clung to that thought, alone beneath the black waters.

CHAPTER 7
DISASTER!

WHEN WENTWORTH awoke from the deep drugged sleep into which Nita had plunged him for his own protection, he found his physician taking his pulse. Dr. Riggs nodded briskly as he rose to his feet.

"You'll be all right now, Dick," he said quietly. "Just rest up for a week, and you'll be fit as a fiddle. You escaped pneumonia by a hair."

Wentworth gazed blankly at the doctor for a long minute, and then the whole circumstance of the situation rushed over him. He rose up from the bed.

"What time is it?" he demanded.

The doctor consulted his watch. "Seven o'clock. Evening. You've had a good fifteen-hour sleep."

"Fifteen hours!" Wentworth echoed. He flung the covers aside, bounded to his feet. His jab at the bell-push brought Jenkyns at a run. His face wrinkled in a delighted smile at sight of Wentworth.

"Where is Miss Nita?" Wentworth asked quickly.

The smile left Jenkyns' face at once. He shook his white head. "She left here about three o'clock in the morning, sir, with Ram Singh. I have heard nothing from either of them."

"Jackson?"

"Not since last night, sir," Jenkyns said heavily.

Wentworth pressed down an oath of dismay. What was it

Nita had said just before he fell under the influence of the drugs in the car?

"I promise you your work shall go on!"

With feverish hands, Wentworth began to dress. He was not even aware that the doctor had left.

"Do you know where Miss Nita went?" he demanded of Jenkyns, with harshness creeping into his voice.

"I only know, sir," Jenkyns said miserably, "that Ram Singh spent some time in the supply room and left with a very heavy load on his back."

Wentworth was rapidly knotting his tie. He snatched double shoulder holsters from his closet and weighed two heavy automatics in his fists, checked their loading before he dropped them into their clips. He had small doubts as to what Ram Singh and Nita had intended. But had they run into an ambush, as he had, beneath the waters of the East River? And Jackson… Jenkyns came hurriedly in at the doorway.

"Mr. Kirkpatrick to see you, sir," he announced.

Wentworth whipped toward the door. This was all he needed now, to have Kirkpatrick spring some new trap upon him, inspired by the machinations of the Iron Man!

"How many men did he bring this time?" Wentworth demanded harshly.

Kirkpatrick spoke from the hallway behind Jenkyns, "I am quite alone, Dick," he said. "I bring you news that may have meaning to you. I'll confess we can make very little of it. Your cruiser was picked up by the river police today. It was anchored close to the channel off the site of your destroyed home. There was a diving ladder overside. Nita's slippers, at least I assume they are hers, were aboard, but nothing else."

Wentworth stared at Kirkpatrick fixedly, but made no response to the information. It was just as he had feared. Ram Singh and Nita….

"A man answering Ram Singh's description," Kirkpatrick went on, "was picked up by a tug. He has a broken shoulder, and a slight skull fracture, and is unconscious in Bellevue hospital."

Wentworth made a small gesture with his right hand, "Phone the hospital, Jenkyns," he instructed. "You know what to do. All possible attention. Send Dr. Riggs there at once."

Jenkyns bowed and departed and Wentworth faced Kirkpatrick. His face was drawn and cold. "And Jackson?" he asked quietly. "I suppose he has been arrested?"

KIRKPATRICK FACED him with a still face. "It was about Jackson I came to see you, primarily," he said. "He was taken prisoner last night with the body of a murdered policeman in his arms. Apparently, it was his intention to throw the body into the river!"

Wentworth nodded heavily, "I was afraid of that," he said slowly. "I assume full responsibility. The policeman was killed by a robot I encountered off Sutton Place last night. In your present suspicious frame of mind, I was dubious that you would believe that such things as robots existed. Jackson volunteered to remove the body from the vicinity of my wrecked car, and I did not countermand him as I should have. That is the truth of it, Kirk. I give you my word."

Kirkpatrick's own voice was heavy. "I was sure there was an

She felt steel talons
close about her.

explanation," he said slowly. "If you will make that statement to my secretary and sign it, I think we'll get Jackson off in a few days."

Wentworth looked sharply at Kirkpatrick and saw that his friend was trying to make amends for the suspicions of the night before. There was a pleading that Kirk would never voice deep in his frosty blue eyes. Abruptly, Wentworth thrust out his hand.

"Thanks, Kirk," he said. "I know you could make it pretty tough for Jackson. And I think we'd better join forces. These robots are too much for either of us, single-handed. Shall we go to headquarters while I tell you what I know?"

The night was crystal clear, and bitterly cold. Wentworth muffled himself to the ears in a great coat before climbing into Kirkpatrick's car. He was desperately anxious to start out upon Nita's trail, but he had no starting point. If Nita had disappeared, there was no hope that the robot would still lie disabled on the river bottom.

"I had intended to check up on Drexler last night," Wentworth told Kirkpatrick quietly. "The same thought must have occurred to you."

Kirkpatrick looked at him sharply. "Are you sure you didn't pay Drexler a visit?"

"I gather that the Spider did," Wentworth said drily. "And yet I'm inclined to believe in Drexler."

Kirkpatrick nodded reluctantly. "There's a report about the city that people will be safe if they employ Drexler guards," he said. "A number of prominent men have called me about that report. Of the three who were robbed last night, Aaron Smedley at least had been warned to hire Drexler guards!

"Drexler swears he knows nothing of the matter. There is nothing to show that these racketeer threats were made by anyone connected with him… and Drexler voluntarily submitted his books for examination. He admitted that his business had been growing lately by leaps and bounds, that he had been compelled to employ many new men."

"Yet you believe in Drexler, too?" Wentworth asked softly.

Kirkpatrick's jaw set in a stubborn line. "I believe in Drexler," he said. "It's possible someone is using him as a scapegoat. That has happened before this."

Wentworth agreed, and told of his discoveries concerning the robots and of disabling one beneath the river; and of what he feared had happened to Nita.

"You should have notified us, Dick!" Kirkpatrick snapped.

Wentworth smiled slightly, but made no other answer. Kirkpatrick had scarcely been in a tractable mood yesterday.

"So I'd like your men to make all possible efforts to find some trace of Nita," he went on steadily. "And post a guard over Ram Singh to notify us the moment he regains consciousness. It's just possible he may know something. My guess is that Nita insisted on making the dive herself, that she was attacked by robots and Ram Singh dove to her rescue! He was probably disabled by a single blow that broke his shoulder and cracked his skull, and was lucky enough to be picked up."

Kirkpatrick said heavily, "It sums up to this: several hundred thousand dollars worth of damage has been done, a score of people have been brutally murdered—and if the robots decided to march on police headquarters and wipe it out, we could not stop them! Something must be done!"

Wentworth whispered, "Something!"

HIS VOICE died in the whine of the radio in the car. "Sergeant Reams, call headquarters," came the announcer's voice. "Sergeant Reams, call headquarters."

Kirkpatrick stiffened in his seat. It was the code by which headquarters indicated an urgent need to get in touch with him. The driver swung the heavy car to the curb beside a call box and Kirkpatrick leaped to the pavement. Wentworth leaned forward and deliberately tuned the radio to a news broadcast which he knew would be going on at this moment.

"The New York police have a new mystery," said the announcer, "which may or may not be connected with the great steel giants which are destroying property and killing civilians. A rowboat drifting down the East River was picked up today and in it was found a woman's clothing, complete to the last item except for the shoes. Police said that the clothing contained a secret message which would, and I quote, 'enable them to crack the case in twenty-four hours!'"

Wentworth's eyes narrowed as the full impact of the words struck him, and he turned to see Kirkpatrick leaping toward the car. "Get to headquarters fast!" he snapped, grimly. "Those damned fools!"

Wentworth said savagely, "That was madness, Kirk! They gave out on the radio the fact that they had a secret message. Before we can reach there, they may move her!"

Kirkpatrick stared at Wentworth without comprehension. "What in hell are you talking about?"

Wentworth explained rapidly. "Plainly, those must be Nita's clothes! It's a taunt at me, and she was clever enough to plant some message in them. Get me there fast, Kirk. I've got to see for myself what this message is!"

The car was already roaring through the streets, parting traffic with the shriek of its siren. Kirkpatrick massaged his brows with bony fingers. "I see," he said slowly. "I didn't know about that. The news I received was that the Iron Man telephoned a few moments ago to speak to me, and those damned fools let him get away! He's calling again! Dick, this may be the break I've been praying for!"

Wentworth's words were urgent. "It's more apt to be a threat, or extortion. Good luck to you, Kirk, I'll follow Nita's message!"

The heavy car slewed to the curb before police headquarters and Kirkpatrick strode swiftly up the steps. His forehead was knotted into a frown. He needed Dick's help in this struggle that lay ahead, but he knew it would be futile to attempt to interrupt him now. As for Wentworth, a great load had lifted from his heart. He knew at least that Nita was alive, otherwise they would not have submitted her to that indignity to taunt him!

"Where are those clothes?" he demanded sharply.

Kirkpatrick threw an order back at Sergeant Reams and the officer led Wentworth rapidly along the wide lower hall to an office on the first floor.

"Wants to identify them clothes picked out of the river," Reams said curtly. "Commissioner's orders, give him all help."

Wentworth thanked Reams, and the dumpy man with the eye-shade rose laboriously from his seat and began to poke over shelves with grimed fingers. He found a package in fresh brown paper.

Wentworth caught it from his hands and ripped it open. It took only a glance to assure him that the clothing was Nita's. The scent of her perfume lifted to his nostrils and pain clutched at his heart. Nita in the hands of those devils! Forced to this indignity!

"You identify them, hey?" the custodian asked shrilly.

Wentworth jerked his head in affirmative. "The radio mentioned a secret message," he said thickly. "What was it?"

THE MAN cackled. "Funny business, that was. Funniest thing I ever did see. Inside her slip, we found this, and we can't make heads or tails of it, for a fact!"

The man poked among the clothing and brought out an envelope. In an instant, Wentworth had ripped it open… and there tumbled into his hand a fragment of white porcelain and gold, a removable bridge containing an artificial tooth! Wentworth gazed down at the bauble, and his throat closed. He remembered when a gangster, striking at him, had caught Nita in the jaw and knocked out that tooth. Strange, how the memory could close his throat. It was hard to force out words.

"Fastened inside the slip?" he asked, and his voice was a whisper.

"Yes, sir, that's right," the man cackled again, "and if you can make heads or tails out of it, you're a better man than anybody around here!"

Wentworth let the bit of bridgework slide back into the envelope. The muscles stood out in knots on his jaws. No question that Nita meant to convey to him her place of imprisonment, but that fool radio broadcast might already have alarmed the crooks. If they moved her... God, he had no time to lose!

Wentworth swung out of the room, into the hall and Sergeant Reams called his name from the head of the steps. Wentworth ignored it, went into the street and nailed a taxi. He had long ago learned the advantage of having a hideout near police headquarters and he directed the driver to that vicinity now. He flung a ten dollar bill to the front seat.

"I want speed," he said flatly.

He got speed, but once he had to stop the taxi to make a phone call. He put through a call to a friend on a morning newspaper.

"I want to know the whereabouts of an abandoned ferry slip, probably on the Hudson River, and near a bridge," he said rapidly. "My guess would be somewhere near the George Washington Bridge—some ferry put out of business by its opening. Can you get that information for me?"

"As it happens," the newspaper man drawled. "You have come to precisely the right man. I looked up that same information for a lad named Frank Drexler about a month ago."

Wentworth struggled to keep his voice calm. "I don't know the gentleman, but where is that slip?" He knew now that he was on the right track. Nita's message had seemed so painfully clear to him, a bridge fastened to a slip... and she had disappeared in the river. The Hudson River had been a guess, of course, but Nita had fastened the bridgework to the *wrong* side of the slip.

It might mean that he had been interested in the wrong river. It might….

"It's not much of a ferry," the newspaper man was drawling. "Last summer is the first it hasn't operated. Used to run across to Interstate Park, and it's just about a mile above George Washington Bridge. As a matter of fact, it may run again. I seem to remember hearing it had been bought."

"Get the name and have it for me," Wentworth told him. "This is worth money to me, and I'll mail you a check."

The newspaper man sighed, "Insulted again, but I love it!"

Wentworth did not hear him. He was leaping toward the taxi. That inquiry by Drexler was the confirmation he needed. He knew now that he was on the right trail… but thanks to the bungling of the police, it might already be cold! Wentworth forced himself to relax. It was madness that he planned: an open attack on a headquarters of robots, even though he would dare greater than that for Nita's sake.

PRESENTLY, AT a dark corner in a district of slums and gaunt warehouses, Wentworth paid off the taxi driver. He waited impatiently until the machine had whirled a corner, and then he sprinted into the dark mouth of an alley. Half way along its length, there was an incongruous small brick garage, whose door mechanism was operated by a masked beam of black light which Wentworth interrupted at irregularly timed intervals. The doors slid open and Wentworth stepped inside.

Parked there was a replica of the battered coupé which he had used the night before. Wentworth's swift glance assured him that everything was in order and then his eyes quested hurriedly over the garage. They lighted on two old ginger-ale bottles on a shelf and, as Wentworth stared at them, a grim light crept into his eyes. Not a weapon he liked to use, but against such monstrous murderers as these men of steel....

He filled those bottles with gasoline. He twisted a bit of rag about each one then and, tightly corked, laid them beside him as he got behind the wheel. He fought the cold motor to life, emerged into the alley, and drove rapidly across town. The motor moaned with power, and Wentworth crouched fiercely over the wheel. Once his eyes strayed to those two innocuous seeming bottles upon the seat, and when they did, cold fires flamed in their depths. God grant that he would be in time!

The ferry house was a squat monster beside the dark Hudson. The slip was its yawning jaws. Above it, to Southward, the inverted arch of the bridge laid a clear curve of beauty against the stars.

The roadway to the ferry house led under a stone arch that bore railway tracks. Beyond this, a battered coupé huddled like an old woman in the shadows. The black shape that detached from it, and drifted beneath the arch, was equally anonymous, but from under the black hat brim cold eyes surveyed the building. Its spire, that once had held a clock, pointed upward like a warning finger.

Through the archway, the wind moaned on the deep note of a dying man. It caught the tail of a long black cape, flapped it once. When he was nearer, the dilapidated aspect of the building showed more clearly. The doors were locked. In Wentworth's nimble fingers a lock-pick made little of that. The door did not creak as he eased it open, but afterward he stood very still inside, and a cold smile moved the lipless gash of the Spider's mouth.

This old building, abandoned for months, held a trace of heat! It was not that the gaunt waiting room was warm, but there was the smell of heat. Wentworth bent quickly, and his fingers hovered above the cracks in the floor. He nodded alertly. The warmth came from below! So quickly, so easily, he had located the hiding place to which Nita's shrewd message had guided him!

Briskly, his eyes quested over the interior. There was an elevator shaft which led to the upper deck of the ferry house; probably downward also. It would not do for the Spider, and there were no stairs in evidence. He whipped out a shielded flashlight and its radiance flickered and vanished, glowed again. He traveled silently along the walls, then swerved toward the deserted change booths. The opening he sought would be masked, and... in the second change booth, Wentworth stopped. His light burned steadily for a half minute. He had found the trap door he sought.

NITA LAY huddled against the wall of the ferry house, arms and legs bound tightly. She was not given to despair, but her lot seemed almost hopeless. How many hours had passed since the robots had ambushed her on the river bottom? They seemed endless, horrible. Those men within the steel monsters... they had forced to her to strip off her clothing as a taunt to Dick... It still brought a burning flush to her cheeks. Her present garments were inadequate, but she had small thought for bodily discomfort. If only she could hope!

There had been hope for hours after she had smuggled that vague message into her clothing. She had been left here alone with only a single guard, one of the Drexler men in uniform, and it seemed to her that her very thoughts must be summoning Dick. Now—she prayed that he would not come!

A half hour ago, three robots had entered the building. One of them had vanished into the elevator shaft, but the other two stood near the trapdoor that opened into this basement room from above. And Nita knew with a terrible certainty why they waited! They were expecting Dick....

At the thought, Nita saw one of the men in steel turn its head slowly and the blank panes of glass stared at her. It was their utter soullessness that was terrifying. A steel hand motioned to the uniformed guard and he pushed himself wearily to his feet, grinned down at Nita.

"Come on, toots," he said. "Me and you is going places!"

"Where?" Nita demanded.

The guard just grinned, caught her by the arm. "A safe place," he said. "I think somebody is paying us a visit, and the Iron Man don't want you hurt none. Not yet, anyway. Come on!"

With the man's hand gripping her arm, Nita surged to her feet. "I can't walk like this," she said. "Untie my ankles."

The man hesitated, then shrugged and stooped to do as she bid. Nita's eyes flashed to the ceiling, and she saw... the trapdoor begin to lift! The robots saw it, too. Their heads were tilted back, their great steel hands poised just beside the opening.

Nita cried, *"Back, Dick!* Two robots... waiting!"

The guard struck Nita across the mouth with the flat of his

hand. In the same instant, a gun blasted from the ceiling! Nita saw the tongue of flame leap out of the darkness overhead, heard the surprised gasp of the man in front of her! His body jerked and pitched heavily against her, bore Nita to the floor. But Nita did not tear her eyes away from the opening in the ceiling. She cried her warning, but there was no answer. She saw a small flicker of fire up there. Then one of the robots took a single stride forward, and reached up into the darkness with great taloned hands of steel!

With a sob, Nita tried to wrestle free of the slain guard's body. She found that her ankle ropes were loose, and she braced her legs, began to wriggle clear. A curious object sailed downward. For a hysterical moment, she thought that she was mistaken. It seemed to her that the thing that plummeted down toward the upturned head of the robot was an ordinary bottle with flaming rags knotted about its base!

There was only that glimpse, then the bottle struck the face of the robot, and burst. That was all for a moment, and then, suddenly, the robot was a tower of flames! Liquid fire dripped down its sides and burned fiercely on the steel legs. The head, shoulders and chest of the robot were blotted out in leaping flames!

FOR A moment the robot stood there, motionless, hands reaching through that trapdoor, and then the thing staggered backward. She had heard them speak before, through the diaphragm magnifier that was hidden somewhere about the great body, but she had never heard such a sound as this. It was a scream of absolute terror, its volume stunning, in this enclosed space. It was as if a ship's siren could take on the qualities of a human voice!

A sob pushed up into Nita's throat as she finally fought her way clear of the guard's body and staggered to her feet. She had been mad to doubt Dick. He had found a way to defeat the robots! The second monster was not waiting to battle against the flame bomb. Instead, it wheeled so quickly that it reeled off-balance against the wall. The battering ram of its shoulder cracked a gaping hole in the concrete, but it staggered on. It came straight toward her!

In terror, Nita turned to flee, and in that moment she saw a figure drop swiftly through the trapdoor, and hang there by one hand—a figure in a kiting black cape. Flat and mocking laughter poured from its lips, and in its right hand another of those absurd glass bottles was clenched. The rags at its base were flaming. Behind him, the other robot beat at its flaming armor, the blows dinning drum beats in rhythm to those awful screams. They were suddenly muffled, almost childlike, and Nita knew that the heat had disabled the amplifier. It was a human voice she heard now.

But the robot that remained on its feet was almost upon her. Nita gasped and turned to run. If it caught her... Dick would be beaten! He could not use the flame bomb! Even as the thought struck her, Nita stumbled, pitched helplessly to the floor. The next instant, the monster was upon her. She felt the steel talons close about her, wrench her aloft.

Her senses reeled dizzily, but she fought for sanity. Somehow, she must contrive to break free, to give Dick his chance! Her eyes quested frantically toward the trapdoor! Dick had not yet dropped to the floor. Instead, he swung in mid-air, now dangling from a length of web. He was driving, feet-foremost straight at the robot who held her prisoner—and then Nita remembered! She remembered that a third robot was hidden in the elevator shaft!

Even as the thought flashed across her mind, she saw the monster heave itself into sight, saw the great taloned hands reach for Wentworth where he swung.

"Behind you, Dick!" Nita cried. "Oh, look behind you!"

Wentworth twisted in mid-air. With a final swing upon the web, he hurled himself into space and landed lightly against the wall. And in the same instant, he hurled his bomb—straight into the face of the second robot!

As if that were the moment her own captor had awaited, Nita felt herself falling! The Spider had no more bombs, and the robot wanted both hands to close the battle. While Nita was still falling, the robot turned and plunged straight toward Wentworth! And now he had only powerless guns—and his wits.

TWO OF the robots were out of the fight. They battled with fires that were spreading. Over the head of the first monster, Nita saw that the tinder-dry flooring of the ferry-house had caught! In a space of minutes, this whole building would be a raging inferno! But Wentworth paid all these things no heed. He was crouched against the concrete wall, his hands empty at his side, waiting for the charge of the robot!

Nita had been badly shaken by her fall, but she struggled to her feet. She threw a frightened glance toward the two flame-wrapped robots, toward the spreading fire that was rapidly eating into the ancient timbers.

"Run, Dick!" she cried. "There is a door at the back. At water level. We can get away!"

Wentworth's voice, reaching out to her, was cold and crisp. "Go there," he ordered quietly. "I'll join you shortly!"

As he finished speaking, the robot struck at him with a taloned hand. Wentworth… was not there. He darted sideways and around the robot, and then Nita saw for the first time that a length of his silken web dangled from his hand! She knew the power of that cord which, scarcely larger than a pencil, would lift a thousand pounds with ease. But it would be no more than cotton string to this monster of steel. Surely, Dick did not expect to bind the robot!

Once more, the robot struck down at Wentworth, and stepped into the noose. The Spider snapped it tight about the jointed ankles. Now, he raced in narrowing circles about the robot, throwing loop after loop of the powerful silken rope about the monster's legs!

"Get to the door!" Wentworth ordered again.

"The right hand, Dick!" Nita cried. "It's getting ready to shoot with those fingers!"

Wentworth's head snapped toward the monster, and he flung himself aside just in time. He whipped out a gun, and tried to duplicate his previous feat of putting a bullet down the barrel of the robot's ingenious gun, but the thing's hand moved too swiftly. Frantically, Wentworth threw a knot into the silken line, then he whirled toward Nita.

"Out the door!" he cried. "Quickly! This building will collapse any minute!"

Nita moved toward the door, trying to open it with her bound hands, but her eyes riveted with an awful fascination on the robot. It swung a great arm about to bring the gun to bear again. It took a stride, and the silken line drew taut about its ankles. Nita saw the silk draw thin, saw a strand snap! But the other wrappings held, and the stride was only half-completed.

At the same instant, behind the monster, Wentworth thrust up both his automatics and emptied them in a swift drum-roll against the back of the creature's head. The lead would not penetrate, but each one struck with the force of a half-ton. Combined with the hobbling silk about its ankles, the blow was enough. The robot tottered, tried to keep its balance, and pitched violently forward to the concrete floor!

IT WAS an incredible spectacle, the fall of that giant, like the death of some great redwood, pierced by the lumberman's saw. Under the impact, the concrete floor cracked like ice, and fragments of gray stone spun into the air. The jar loosened the timbers overhead and a great flaming beam wrenched free and speared down into the basement! Nita had the door open now, and she called out to Wentworth, but he stood by the fallen monster. He was bending over the helmet which his bullets had battered.

"Hurry, Dick!" Nita called. "He may be stunned by the fall, but it's no more than that. Come on, before he revives!"

Instead of answering, Wentworth flung himself suddenly

astride the fallen giant, and his hands tore at the base of the helmet.

"Get outside!" Wentworth called once more. "I'll be with you in a moment!"

As he spoke, the helmet came loose in his hands and Nita saw the lolling head of a man. He wore a curious sort of crash helmet, but blood seeped from his nostrils and he was completely unconscious. She stared incredulously at this human being who, encased in steel, was so ponderous, so terrible. He seemed as defenseless as an oyster stripped of its shell. As she watched, Wentworth whipped up an automatic and struck once, with carefully calculated force, at the base of the man's skull. Then he raced toward her.

In an instant, he slashed the bonds from her wrists. His arm flung about her, he sprang from the doorway to a narrow wooden walkway that skirted the black, oily waters of the slip. A hundred yards offshore, a barge piled high with gravel floated high in the water, and Wentworth's eyes raked it as he reached for a wooden ladder that led to the shore.

"That barge!" he cried. "It floats too high in the water to be loaded like that with gravel! That's how these monsters travel! An airlock under the water would do it. No wonder I lost them in the East River!"

Nita was sobbing, "Dick, oh Dick! I bungled things terribly, didn't I? But I was so worried about you!"

Wentworth laughed sharply. "On the contrary, my dear," he cried. "You have solved the case!"

He leaped over the verge of the shore, reached down to drag

129

Nita upward, and she looked beyond him. Her breath broke with a gasp.

"Oh, Dick!" she cried. "Look, the police! Kirkpatrick!"

Wentworth swore as he set her feet on dry land, threw an arm about her waist. "I should have known better than to ask that newspaper man a question without satisfying his curiosity," he said. "That's what did it! Listen, dear, go to Kirkpatrick at once, but don't mention that barge out there! Tell him everything else. Understand?"

Nita's white face was turned toward him. "Yes, Dick, but what are you going to do?"

Wentworth set her from him, and his laughter rang out clearly, briefly. "I'm going to smash this case wide open!" he cried softly.

POLICE WERE running toward them now. Kirkpatrick's challenge rang out harshly. "Surrender, Spider! You're covered by a dozen guns!"

Wentworth laughed once more. He whirled… and ran back toward the blazing ferry house! Nita gasped, and her hands reached out to him, and then she did a daring thing! She stepped squarely between Wentworth and Kirkpatrick, between him and the line of policemen with lifted guns. And she turned her face toward Dick!

The ferry house was a soaring spire of flame. The angry crackling of the fire was like thunder and, even in the bitter cold, the heat struck like a mallet. Nita wavered on her feet, and suddenly Kirkpatrick was beside her. He flung a strong arm about her waist, leveled his revolver… and Dick was out of sight!

"After him!" Kirkpatrick snapped out his orders. "Block that slip in case he tries to leave by water. If he wants to commit suicide in that fire…" His voice trailed off.

Nita stood rigidly within the curve of Kirkpatrick's arm. She was trembling, but it was not from the cold. She had heard no splash of water after Dick had ducked over the edge of the slip. In heaven's name, had he gone back into that inferno? Nita lifted her hands to her lips.

"I hope he escapes," she whispered. "He is a very gallant man."

Kirkpatrick made no answer, but there was worry about the stern corners of his lips. "Surely, no man could live in that building," he muttered. "It will collapse in a moment! Back there! *Get back!*" As he spoke, a section of the roof crashed inward, and a flying brand flew out to hiss into the black waters. The policemen lining the banks of the slip drew back, vanquished by the heat.

"He went inside, Commissioner!" one of them called. "He's done for!"

Nita bit down a sob. It wasn't possible. Not Dick, who had been so strong and confident beside her a moment before! And yet… there had been no splash! A choked cry lifted into Nita's throat, and Kirkpatrick swore at her side. With a final, thunderous roar, the entire ferry house caved in upon itself! Afterward, there was only the twisting, lifting spirals of dark smoke and eager, exultant flames. Of the Spider, there was no sign at all.

CHAPTER 8
LAST WARNING!

NITA SCARCELY heard Kirkpatrick's orders as he sent men along the shore line to keep watch on the black waters. She was only vaguely aware that a cloak had been thrown about her shoulders. This disaster, after her rescue had raised her hopes so high, sapped the last of her vitality. It was only much later, when the ferry house had at last caved in upon itself, that she remembered Dick Wentworth had warned her not to mention the connection of the barge offshore with the ferry house.

At the memory, she glanced toward the barge—and it was gone! Frantic thoughts darted through her mind, but she dared not ask a question lest it draw attention to the fact that the barge had been there. If Dick had mentioned the barge, then he had had some plan! Slight as were her reasons for hope, Nita clung to them. She could even smile a little when Kirkpatrick came striding toward her, crisp and grave as always.

"Two of those robots in the ruins," he said curtly. "Can't find anything else."

"Two robots," Nita repeated after him, "but—" She cut her words off. There had been three. Perhaps that, too, she was not to tell Kirkpatrick.

"But what?" Kirkpatrick demanded harshly.

Nita shook her head. "I didn't know that they had been killed," she said slowly. "The Spider attacked them with some bottles, filled with gasoline I think, and wrapped in flaming cloths. But I didn't know they were enough to kill the robots!"

Kirkpatrick uttered a sharp exclamation. "By the heavens, I believe the Spider has shown us the way!" he cried. "They used bombs like that in the Spanish Civil War... against tanks, you know. They might work! Heaven knows, we'll have to find something and find it fast!"

A despair in Kirkpatrick's voice pulled Nita's attention wholly to him, and she placed a hand upon his arm. "Is it... very bad, Stanley?" she asked.

Kirkpatrick's lips stretched into a thin straight line. "That hardly describes it," he said slowly. "Before we got this tip-off from a newspaper man, I had a call from the Iron Man. He said he would 'give us a lesson tonight.' Tomorrow, if the police did not voluntarily surrender their jobs to the Drexler agency, headquarters and all major officials would be destroyed!"

"Then you've arrested Drexler at last!" Nita cried.

Kirkpatrick shook his head heavily. He was leading her now toward the stone archway and his parked car. "There is no evidence against him," he said curtly. "My men have been following him day and night; his books and office have been thrown open to us. There is no proof!"

Nita's laughter was sharp and taunting. "And you say there is no place for such men as the Spider!" she said ironically. "You know the man is guilty, and you cannot arrest him even to prevent wholesale murder!"

Kirkpatrick shook his head and stubbornness squared his jaw.

"In the end, the law always wins," he said curtly. "It may muddle along, but the law always wins."

"Thanks to the Spider," Nita said quietly. "Where is Dick, do you know?"

Kirkpatrick glanced at her as he handed her into the rear of his police limousine. The police driver saluted respectfully, and Nita repeated her question.

"He'll be worried about me," she insisted. "I want to communicate with him at the first possible moment."

KIRKPATRICK'S VOICE was impatient. "Dick left me at headquarters," he said shortly. "I don't know his whereabouts any more than I know those of the Spider. I'll drop you at your home, Nita. Meanwhile, will you kindly tell me just what happened? I might learn something that will help to trap the Iron Man and these steel monsters of his!"

"What, without legal evidence, Kirk?" Nita asked, her voice low with mockery, while her mind raced over the events of her captivity. Dick had told her to relate everything except his suspicions regarding the barge. She began to talk rapidly, but her thoughts were not on what she said. She had not lied when she said she wished to get in touch with Wentworth at once. He must be told that the Iron Man planned to inflict a "lesson" upon the city tonight. At the thought of that, Nita felt tension crawl through her body. There was so little she, or anyone else, could do—except the Spider!

Nita knew a new humbleness of spirit at thought of the man she loved. At such moments, he seemed more than human. His keen brain flashed always ahead to the true hidden meaning of criminal problems, and found the way to defeat them. He had needed only to glance at the high-riding barge to guess the secret of its use. Her despair of a short while before seemed a disloyalty now. Dick would not have dashed back into the building had he not a plan... and not a mere plan for escape. Wentworth had gone once more to battle giants!

Nita fell silent, dropped her head gravely. Her hands were clasped hard in her lap, as if in prayer.

"What you say doesn't help much, Nita," Kirkpatrick said. His voice sounded angry and puzzled. "If only I knew how they move under the water. Always, they seem to return to the water on the East River, yet their headquarters apparently was here! Well, we have to thank the Spider for destroying this stronghold!"

"Instead of thanking him," Nita said, scornfully, "you will chalk up two more murders to his name. Torch murders, would you call them? And the destruction of the ferry house! Tell me, Stanley, will your legal conscience permit you to use the gasoline bombs? Or must more people die under their attacks?"

"They are outside the law," Kirkpatrick said sternly.

Nita sighed and turned her gaze to the road ahead. The car had left the West Side highway and was tooling along Riverside Drive. The high viaduct that spanned the valley at 125th Street was just ahead. She would be home soon, but how could she communicate with Dick?

"Had it occurred to you?" she asked Kirkpatrick slowly, "that perhaps this 'lesson' may be an attack on yourself? The promise of an attack later, might merely have been meant to disarm you for the present."

Kirkpatrick nodded stiffly. "I am taking all possible precautions now," he said. "As soon as I can reach headquarters, I'll have some of those gasoline bombs prepared... You must be careful, Nita. It's quite obvious that the Iron Man is intent on destroying you and... Dick."

NITA SMILED, and there was tenderness in the curve of her lips, and pride, too. So many monsters had tried to destroy Dick. One and all, they had been vanquished, though she admitted with a thrill of fear, that he had never fought such impregnable creatures as these men of steel. Her eyes quested longingly ahead as the limousine swung out on the viaduct. If only she could be sure that Dick was safe now... Suddenly her hand gripped Kirkpatrick's arm.

"In heaven's name, Stanley," she gasped. "Look! *Look at that Fifth Avenue bus!*"

A startled oath sprang to Kirkpatrick's lips, and he leaned forward to snap an order at the driver, but it was already too late! Nita saw the things that happened as a wildly fantastic dream. The huge double-decked bus was careening wildly across the viaduct, and stretched out upon its upper deck, crushing the steel framework beneath their colossal weight, were two of the robots! Nita saw that the powerful arm of one of the monsters was stretched down into the cabin, and that a steel forefinger was pointed at the head of the frantic driver. There was no other living being aboard the bus!

As Kirkpatrick shouted to the driver to whirl the limousine

about and retreat, the bus shrieked in a furious turn and came to a halt just in front of the police car! The robots stepped to the pavement and heaved the bus over so that it blocked the viaduct. Then they turned and came toward the police commissioner's car!

The driver barely succeeded in stopping the car before it collided with the wreckage of the bus. He was fighting now to back out of range of those two oncoming terrors. Kirkpatrick had his revolver in his fist. He opened a compartment and seized a hand grenade, but Nita knew grenades were futile.

"Get out and run," Kirkpatrick said sharply. "I'm the one they want, Nita. I can hold them for a while!"

"Come with me!" Nita cried. "They can't move very fast, and if we can dodge their bullets, we can still get away!"

She batted open the door on her side, but in the same instant the robot reached the car. Its steel hand smashed against the door, wedged it fast. The other robot reached through the front window as Kirkpatrick's gun blasted furiously. His futile bullets screamed off the metal of the steel talons. The driver screamed terribly through a single tearing instant. The hand clamped on his shoulder—and pulled!

The driver's scream soared to an incredible thinness. His head had caught against the top of the door as the hand dragged him through the open window, but the hand was inexorable. The scream broke off and there was a dull snapping sound. Afterward, Nita saw a blue clad body hurtle through the air toward the railing of the viaduct and disappear into the darkness beyond.

"Down on the floor," Kirkpatrick snapped.

She saw his hands wrench the pin from the grenade, toss it outside. The explosion made the heavy limousine jump. It seemed to drive in her ear-drums, and immediately thereafter she heard a scream such as had pierced her brain once before—when Wentworth had smashed his flame-bomb against one of the robots.

CAUTIOUSLY, NITA lifted her head, and she saw an incredible thing! One of the robots had turned on the other, had moved up behind the steel monster while he was torturing the driver! Nita's gasp brought Kirkpatrick up from the floor. He was clutching another grenade, but his grip remained frozen. He, too, stared at the bizarre spectacle. The robot who had killed the driver was pitching forward on its face, still screaming. The second robot had stepped up behind it and seized its ankles in mighty fists... and lifted it clear of the pavement!

Even as Nita watched, the viaduct quivered under the impact of the thing's fall. She saw the flooring of the viaduct crack and give way. Paving blocks disappeared through a gaping hole in the pavement... and the scream stopped! But the second robot was not through. It stooped above its fallen comrade, and got a new grip. She heard a slow creaking sound, as when terrific strain is put upon a hoist, and then... and then the robot lifted the fallen monster high over its head. A stride, another... and the robot went sailing through the air toward the railing! In exactly the arc that the already dead police driver had described, the steel monster hurtled through space. The crash of its fall was like the explosion of a great bomb. And the second robot turned back toward the police car.

"I could not destroy him sooner," it said in a booming voice. "There was no time for a battle and I had to take him unawares. I am sorry for the driver's death!"

Kirkpatrick pushed to his feet, flung wide the door of the car and stepped courageously to the pavement. His fist was wrapped about the grenade, clenched to throw. Nita gasped, and flung herself forward to seize that wrist!

"Don't throw!" she cried. "Don't you recognize that voice? It's… it's the Spider!"

Kirkpatrick's wrist stiffened in her grasp, and the two stood staring up into the blankly unfeeling face of the steel monster. The yelp of sirens was thin in the air behind them and Nita's head whipped that way. Two Fifth Avenue buses were roaring toward them, while motorcycle police cleared a path with their sirens. A machine gun stammered from its motorcycle mount, but the bullets screamed overhead.

"Back in the car, Commissioner!" a voice trumpeted from the police. "Give us a clear target!"

The robot did not glance toward the attack. Incongruous in a great steel fist, Nita saw a slim platinum cigarette lighter which she recognized with a throb. Even as she gasped, the robot bent and pressed the base of that lighter to the break in the pavement of the viaduct, and when he had straightened, the gleaming red seal of the Spider shone there! But the robot was talking….

"The 'lesson' which the Iron Man intends to inflict tonight," the Spider's amplified voice boomed, "will be inflicted on the subway at Forty-second and Fifth Avenue. I will do what I can to prevent it, Kirkpatrick. Have your men armed with flame bombs, but if you value the salvation of your city, do not let them throw at me until after the battle! I will mark myself!"

As he spoke, the steel hand lifted again and, on the forehead of the helmet, he imprinted the seal of the Spider!

"Hurry, Kirkpatrick," he said once more. "I do not know how much time is left to us!"

WITH THE words, the robot turned away toward the railing of the viaduct. There was a shout, and a roar of motors behind and the Fifth Avenue buses, police at their wheels, charged toward the retreating form of steel. Nita cried out, and flung herself at Kirkpatrick.

"Stop them!" she cried. "Don't you realize he is your only hope!"

Kirkpatrick wrenched himself free, sprang toward the car, but Nita flung herself straight forward—into the path of the onrushing buses! It was only when she heard Kirkpatrick's voice boom out over the loudspeaker of his car that she realized he had taken the more effective way to stop that charge.

"Stop!" he bellowed above the roar of the charging motors. "Stop those buses! Kirkpatrick's orders!"

Nevertheless, Nita stood firm, straight and slender in the path of those juggernauts. Through long seconds, it did not seem possible that they could stop in time, but finally they grumbled to a halt within feet of where she stood. Angry police poured from them. Men sprang from the motorcycles and charged toward her, shouting, but Nita looked toward the railing of the viaduct

There was a great gaping tear in the steel balustrade, but of the robot, there was no sign at all. One of the men darted to the verge, and began blasting bullets down into the darkness.

"It's climbing down the pillar!" he shouted. "Circle around! We can still catch it on the streets below!"

INSIDE THE steel shell he had captured in the burning wreckage of the ferry house, Wentworth made no effort to avoid the bullets rained upon him from above. Their hammering was like a trip-hammer in the curved top of the helmet, but all his attention was concentrated on the stupendous task of managing the robot in a climb down the steel pillar of the viaduct. He was crouched in the body of the monster, on an upholstered saddle to which he was strapped like an airplane pilot. His feet rode in stirrups which controlled the movements of the legs, and there were two hand grips before him by which he could direct the arms. Other specialized movements were controlled by a series of push-buttons set like a miniature typewriter keyboard before him.

Below and around him, there was the whirr of machinery which he had not stopped to examine and the oily stench of it was strong in his nostrils. The noise was terrific, deafening. And he needed the crash helmet which he had stripped from the man slain inside the ferry house. The lurching of the robot was impossible to control, and his head banged again and again on the steel sides of the monster.

His plans were carefully made. He would find a truck here

in the heavy traffic that filed toward the ferry and, in it would make his dash to Fifth and Forty-second.

How many robots would be sent to destroy the subway he could not guess. He only knew that, by means of the small radio receiver within the robot, he had received orders with another of the monsters to destroy Kirkpatrick and, afterward, to go to the appointed place of the subway attack. If there were many others there, and this double duty seemed to indicate that the whole force was involved—it was a question how much he could accomplish against them, even in this powerful robot!

Wentworth heard the thin wailing of sirens as he reached the earth beneath the viaduct and looked slowly about him through the great blank eyes of the robot. Men were running from him in screaming terror, abandoning their automobiles in panic. He saw a driver leap from an oil truck and, in the sheer blindness of his terror, dart almost straight toward him!

AS GENTLY as possible, Wentworth picked up the man, and spoke to him through the microphone which dangled before his lips. "I won't hurt you," he said, and tried to make his voice soft. "I need transportation. We are going back to your truck. I will sit astride it, and you will drive me to Fifth Avenue and Forty-second Street. Understand?"

He was holding the man high before the blank eyes of the robot, and he could see the writhing terror of the man's face, but the driver managed some sort of affirmative. Wentworth had never ceased to advance, and now he eased the man into the cab of his truck, swung astride of it.

Wentworth's gaze ranged ahead down Fifth Avenue, seeking

some trace of the steel monsters he must destroy. His ear-phones were silent save for the ceaseless rasping of police orders. Twice, he heard Kirkpatrick's clear voice and heard the command to manufacture flame bombs!

Abruptly, he snapped to attention. Far down the length of Fifth Avenue, he caught the glint of street lights on steel. At first it was no more than that, and then his straining eyes made out the regular ranks of the robots, marching up Fifth Avenue. There were only six of them now, behind the taller figure of the Iron Man, but they were enough!

"Faster!" he shouted at the driver. "Faster, man!"

The bellow of his voice beat back into his ears, and he saw windows shiver and crash inward at the concussion of the sound! And then, dead ahead of him, two trucks swung out of a side street! For an instant, they clashed together and then they straightened out, completely closing Fifth Avenue. Wentworth surged forward as the power brakes of the oil truck took hold. Then, with a titanic collision, the three trucks slammed together and Wentworth felt himself falling!

Twice, he had seen robots fall from slighter distance than this and each time the men inside them had been knocked out! Even as the thought flashed across his mind, he saw oil gush from the torn side of the truck, saw flame flick upward. The robot, carrying Wentworth with it, plunged toward a lake of flaming oil!

CHAPTER 9
BATTLE OF THE GIANTS

FALLING TOWARD that lake of burning oil, Wentworth did the only thing he could. He braced himself rigidly against the strap that bound him and thrust the arms and legs of the robot rigidly forward. If he plunged into the flames, he was done for. There was small chance that he would be able to extract himself from the suit before the terrific heat overpowered him, even if the police would allow him opportunity.

An eternity passed while he plunged toward the street, but the weight of the outthrust arms and legs decided the issue. They pointed downward and it was in that position, he fell to the street. The flames splashed toward him, coated his limbs almost to the joints. For an instant longer, Wentworth held motionless until sure that the robot was balanced, and then he straightened and plunged toward the sidewalk!

He held the hands of the monster straight out to the sides, and the flames flapped back from them, away from his body. On the legs, the polished surface of the steel shed the oil downward. So the Spider, flaming, hurled himself toward the scene of battle.

Wentworth turned the robot's head and peered at the traffic, spotted a bus from which the passengers fled in terror, and suddenly he saw how he could attack the robots! Wentworth lunged toward the bus, pointing a gun finger at the driver.

"Drive down Fifth!" he shouted, "or you die!"

Left-handed, Wentworth reached out to one of the light standards that rose on each side of the avenue. A single wrench-

144

ing heave, and the iron post snapped off in his hand. The next instant, he had thrown himself prone atop the bus. He dangled a hand to point into the cab, and the truck lurched forward beneath him. Grimly, then, Wentworth straightened atop the bus, while it roared down the avenue.

He could see the robots more clearly now. They were passing Forty-first street. It would be a close thing whether the robots or Wentworth reached Forty-Second street first.

"Faster!" Wentworth shouted. "Faster! Pass the robots on the left! And do not be afraid. *I am the Spider!*"

His voice boomed hollowly down the street and it seemed to him that after that the bus was driven more positively, more steadily.

At the last moment two of the robots understood and tried to dodge aside, but Wentworth was ready! The iron post whirled like a polo mallet and crashed against the helmet of the foremost giant. There was a hollow clang, and the shock of the impact ran along the iron club… and the helmet was driven in as if it were no more than papier-mâché! A shout of triumph burst from Wentworth's lips again, and he swung the war club a second time before the bus rushed past in that fierce charge.

"Turn!" Wentworth shouted. "Turn the bus and charge again!"

HE TWISTED about to peer backward. Three of the robots were down after his headlong charge, but it was apparent one of them had only been overturned. Already, with stiff movements, it was climbing to its feet again. Wentworth was almost unseated as the bus whipped around a corner and headed for

Madison Avenue. He set the robot legs more tightly about the truck body and braced himself for the next curve.

When the bus rounded back into Fifth Avenue, Wentworth saw that a line of blue clad police was advancing cautiously toward the robots. Guns were blasting futilely in their fists, and Wentworth could not determine whether they also carried flame bombs. It was a vain gesture they were trying if they carried any lesser arms, but Wentworth thrilled to the courage of the men advancing in the face of certain death. He saw the Iron Man wade toward them, deliberately crush one of the helpless police underfoot! A scooping hand picked up another and dangled him, screaming in mid-air!

"Faster!" Wentworth shouted. "Straight for that big one!"

The engine of the bus strained mightily—and then Wentworth saw what defense the robots would use against him! Two of them had caught up the steel giants he had slain, and held them poised above their heads! Too late, Wentworth recognized the peril and tried to shout a warning to the driver. He whirled the massive club about his head and let it fly straight at the nearest of the enemy! It struck solidly, and he saw the armor plate of the robot buckle inward at the moment it launched its awful missile! That robot, hurtling through the air, did not fly true. It struck in the path of the bus and Wentworth gripped hard with both hands to withstand the shock. An instant later, the bus struck. Its rear wheels lifted high into the air and, at the same instant, the second hurled robot crashed against it!

The double impact jarred Wentworth savagely against the sides of his steel prison. His head, inside the crash helmet swam dizzily, but his hand-hold was not jarred loose. He sat through a long moment atop the wreckage of the bus and saw three of the remaining robots stride toward him. With a gasp of thankfulness, he saw that his club had penetrated the chest of the third victim. It lay flat upon its back, with the steel post jutting from it like a spear. But the Iron Man himself still dangled the policeman from his hand. As Wentworth shook himself free of the lethargy of shock, he saw the Iron Man clamp another hand on the helpless policeman's head and… and *pull!*

His senses still reeling, he hoisted the robot to its feet just as three robots charged upon him! Somehow, Wentworth floundered aside from that first attack. Three strides took him to another light standard and he wrenched it loose and whirled it fiercely about his head!

As he slashed down once more, a police car screamed around the corner behind the robots. Wentworth saw something that glittered sail through the air, something that flapped a thin trailer of flame behind it—and then the object struck the rearmost robot and flames splashed over the steel armor!

LAUGHTER PUMPED from Wentworth's lips, the thin and mocking laughter of the Spider. Two other robots remained. One of them turned upon the police car, and it lashed out with a kick of its tremendous foot. There were screams from the car, and then the machine was overturned. An instant later, the wreckage burst into flames.

But Wentworth was once more in motion. The iron club slashed through the air and caught the robot across the back of the helmet. The casque split like a ripe melon and the robot pitched to the street. The remaining robot wheeled and began to retreat! For an instant Wentworth hesitated, then he sprang toward the wreckage of the police car. With a swift surge of power, he set the machine right side up again, saw two men wrench themselves free and rush to safety.

The two robots that remained stood side by side before the entrance of the library. As Wentworth marched toward them, hands aswing at his side, he saw the Iron Man stoop toward one of the great stone lions before the library! Before Wentworth guessed his purpose, the lion was hurled at him!

It was the handicap of the robot monsters that they could not move swiftly. Wentworth pivoted, took a long step to the side, and the granite lion struck the pavement and shattered like a bomb. A huge fragment smashed against the left knee of Wentworth's robot and knocked the leg out from under him. Outflung hands caught Wentworth as he went down, and he was upon his feet before the two robots could destroy him. But when he moved forward the left leg dragged. Yet, as the smaller robot tried to wrench the other lion loose, Wentworth was upon it!

Wentworth's mechanical hands seized upon one arm of the robot, and he began to twist! For an instant, the other strained fiercely, then it lifted the finger gun and blasted at the glass eyes of Wentworth's robot! The bullet did not penetrate, but the glass frosted over. Wentworth did not change his stance, but kept up the inexorable twisting. He heard a shriek of sirens and guessed that a new squad of bomb-throwers had come. A blow on the side of the helmet jarred him to his spine, and he twisted the robot head to see the Iron Man himself.

It was a smashing down blow of the fist that had struck on the helmet. The seams of it had started under that impact, and Wentworth knew that another would drive the metal into his skull! A shout of defiance lifted to Wentworth's lips. He flung all the power of his robot into a final wrench on the metal arm of the other, and swung toward the Iron Man!

The Iron Man staggered backward and the second blow miscarried. There was a shriek of tortured metal, and Wentworth found that he had torn loose the steel arm of the robot! It was the monster's fall that had driven the Iron Man backward!

Once more, the laughter of the Spider rang through the street! He lifted the steel arm like a club and struck downward. In the wreckage of the robot at his feet, nothing stirred and he lifted his head then toward the Iron Man himself! The Iron Man was fleeing!

GRIMLY, WENTWORTH pursued. He fought the crippled mechanism of his robot, saw a flaming bottle-bomb sail past just in front of him! What the devil—couldn't the police see he was fighting their battle for them?

"Fools!" he cried, "I am your friend!" His voice beat back on his own ears, but did not sound outside the steel casque. During the fight, the speech mechanism had been smashed! And the Iron Man already was turning the corner a half block away!

Wentworth drove the robot into a run—a killing task. Each stride drove the steel feet crackling into the pavement; each shortened stride of the left leg almost threw him, but he persisted. He felt warmth upon his back and knew that a flame-bomb must have burst there. His clenching teeth bit out curses, but he drove on violently, rounded the corner.

He stopped short then, staring in frustrated anger. The shell of the Iron Man lay prostrate upon the pavement—but the master criminal had fled!

Dimly, behind him, Wentworth heard the triumphant shout of the police and he felt the minor shock of another flame-bomb bursting against his back!

Blindly, Wentworth swung about. Without hesitation, he strode toward the high door of an office building on his right, and crashed through the metal framework with a single stride.

Swiftly, Wentworth's eyes swept over the interior. Double bronze doors opened into a bank entrance. He reached the doors, tore them open, and stumbled in and shut them. He eased the robot to a squatting position against the doors. He could count on its enormous weight to hold them shut for a few moments. He reached out then for the fastenings of the helmet.

They were hot to the touch, scorched his fingers, but finally drove the helmet free. In the same instant, he freed himself from the straps that held him and hurled himself head-foremost from the imprisoning oven of the armor! He struck the floor on his shoulders, came tumbling to his feet. Somewhere near him, glass crashed and he heard the heavy hammer of police guns, closer.

The Spider darted along the wall, raced for the rear door that he knew must open into a hall. He made it just ahead of the police who were racing to shut that exit. He plunged down cellar steps. The black cape kited out from his shoulders.

It was a work of minutes to find a way out of the cellar, to dart into a side street. Even so, he was only moments ahead of the police as he commandeered a taxi whose driver gaped in awe, ten yards away. Wentworth ground the accelerator to the floor and whipped about in a violent U-turn. He was flashing past the corner before the police could organize, and he had gained three blocks before he heard the first yelp of the sirens!

WENTWORTH KNEW where he was going, but there was a desperate need for haste. His only chance of proving what he knew to be a fact was to catch the Iron Man before he had the opportunity to remove the traces of his activity. And the police would give him so little time; this taxi was so damnably slow.

When presently he whirled toward the East River, sharp laughter burst from his lips. There was the wall about the Drexler home and there, just turning in through the gate, was a fast-driven sedan! It was too dark for Wentworth to see the man who drove it, but he fought another fraction of speed from the taxi and headed for the fast-closing gates. He caught them an instant before they locked, ripped one entirely free from its hinges. Ahead of him, the sedan was sliding into the garage. Those doors were swifter. They had slid into place before Wentworth could reach them, but he did not hesitate.

In an instant, he had leaped from the driver's seat and was racing, not toward the garage, but toward the house itself! His shoulder drove inward an ancient door, and he reeled across the room, to the stairs that led to the basement!

He cleared the basement stairs in two long leaps, cut toward the steel door that closed off the wine cellar. He checked there for an instant to manipulate the lock, and then he swung it wide.

He flicked on the light in the wine cellar—and out of the darkness, a robot reached for him!

Blinded though Wentworth was by the instantaneous flash of the lights, he caught a glimpse of that steel-taloned hand as it streaked toward his feet! Wentworth sprang convulsively into the air, felt the jerk as the talons bit into the tail of his cape, and then he was hurtling through the air, toward the robot.

Wentworth had no hope of knocking the robot off of his feet, but for the Spider, police hard on his heels, there could be no retreat. There was only one way, and that was forward! His left arm circled the neck of the robot, he flung his legs high and went over the shoulder of the steel monster to land lightly on his feet in the middle of the wine cellar!

In the same instant, Wentworth wrenched out his automatics, but he did not turn them upon the robot, which was turning to attack him. He knew too well the uselessness of that process. Instead, he pivoted slowly on his heel and his bullets sped true. Each one knocked out the spigot of a wine barrel! In an instant, the ground was drinking in wines.

It took only an instant, and then Wentworth was forced to leap from the path of the robot. A huge foot had lifted to crush him, and a steel fist swung viciously at his head. The fist missed and swept on to bash in the front of a hogshead. There was an instant, eager gush of red wine and Wentworth leaped warily to crouch close against a stone wall in the protection of another wine tun.

Overhead, Wentworth caught the heavy pound of feet and knew that the police already were charging into the house. God,

154

he had so little time! Even now, he was certain to be trapped when the police rushed to the wine cellar. He shifted again and the groping robot crushed another wine tun, released a fresh flood of liquor over the floor.

WITH A taunting laugh, Wentworth leaped into clear view of the robot. His guns were sheathed now, and the robot turned heavily to face him. It took a long stride toward Wentworth and, in the same instant; the Spider sprang into the air. His up reaching hands grasped the asbestos-covered steam pipe well up toward the ceiling, and as he swung there, the robot uttered a muffled shout and reached for him with fiercely powerful hands! At the same instant, Wentworth heard the door at the head of the wine cellar steps wrenched open, and the quick shouts of the police!

There was no time, no time at all. Wentworth ripped an automatic from beneath his arm and blasted lead upward at the ceiling. The light went out in the same instant. There were crazy shouts behind him, then the brilliant beams of flashlights cut the darkness.

To the men grouped on the stairs; to Nita, who stood in helpless terror there beside Kirkpatrick, they showed a curious sight! Wentworth was dangling by one hand from the steam pipes and, as the robot reached for him; he grabbed into the darkness over his head and then stabbed that hand toward the robot! Only Nita saw what he was doing, and a gasp tore at her throat. She saw the black electric wire in his hand, and guessed that the single bullet he had fired had cut that wire in half!

So much she saw, and then there was a blinding flash of blue-white light as the naked tip of the electric wire ground against the steel armor of the robot. Its feet were knee-deep in wine, a perfect ground. There was that moment of intense illumination, and when it was blotted out, the glare of the flashlights were dark by comparison. The robot seemed to leap clear of the earth, and then crash backward into the flood of wine. For a moment longer, the Spider clung to his high perch and then he, too, dropped into the knee-deep wine, harmless now that the broken wire no longer touched the steel robot.

Kirkpatrick was half-way down the stairs. "All right, Spider," he said quietly, "get your hands up!"

Before Kirkpatrick could protest, Wentworth had stooped. With a few deft movements, he loosened the helmet of the robot, and dragged the dead operator into sight. His face was distorted, but Nita looked at it in amazement, even while she was tortured with the certainty of Dick's capture. She had never seen the man.

"A stranger to most of you, eh, gentlemen?" the Spider murmured. "But you know him, Kirkpatrick, and you, Drexler. How about Drexler, senior, there, do you know him?"

Nita was aware then that the two men had moved up behind her, were crowding past her to the stairs, but it was Kirkpatrick who answered.

"Louis Montose," he said in amazement. "But he can't be the Iron Man!"

"You're right," Wentworth said quietly. "He was just a minor crook, who worked for the real villain of the piece, who stands just beside you on the steps!"

157

THE SPIDER

KIRKPATRICK GLANCED to his right, and uttered a disgusted exclamation. "Drexler cannot be guilty!" he said sharply. "I have checked him on every point, and he is in the clear!"

Wentworth smiled, "It is queer what things a man can achieve when he has been a weakling all his life," he said softly, but still in the mocking intonation of the Spider. "It is queer what dreams that sort of life can breed, dreams of *power!* Look to your left, Kirkpatrick, and tell me... what are those red objects in the ears of Drexler's father?"

Kirkpatrick said, emptily, "Drexler's father? Now, *I* know you are mad, Spider! A weak old man...."

"A weakling all his life," Wentworth said softly, "but within a robot, his strength becomes that of a giant. A touch of a lever and he can smash in a building. *What is that in his ears?*"

Kirkpatrick said, in bewilderment, "Why he has some of those rubber stopples used to keep water out of the ears in swimming!"

"Or to reduce the incredible racket those robots make, when you're inside one!" Wentworth threw in. "Also, if you will take off the hat of Drexler senior, you will see there the marks made by the straps of a crash helmet such as this dead man wears!"

Old Drexler's face was suddenly fiery red. He twisted toward his son. "You turned me in, you mealy-mouthed coward!" he said shrilly. "I was doing all this for you, to make you the greatest man in the world, something I never had the strength to do! You—"

Old Drexler whipped up his cane and made a violent swing with it. It just missed his son's head and the old man lost his footing and pitched headlong down the steps! His foot caught in the open work of the stairs and he lay there, head down, hands up thrown and dangling, just touching the wine that was red as spilled blood.

"No, don't touch him!" Wentworth said softly. "He's already dead, as you can see from the blueness of his face. Heart failure, I should judge." As he spoke, he bent forward and pressed the base of his cigarette lighter against the chilling flesh of the dead man's forehead, and when he straightened there glowed there the crimson seal of the Spider!

Inarticulate rage burst in a roar from Drexler's throat. "You killed him, you trickster!" he shouted, and leaped down the steps!

Kirkpatrick shouted, tried to stop Drexler, but it was too late. Kirkpatrick fired a single shot that went wide of its mark, and then the Spider was fleeing across the cellar with Drexler raging behind him. They reached an alcove in the left-hand wall, and Kirkpatrick shouted fiercely.

"Down here, men!" he cried. "And careful! We've trapped the Spider too often to have him get away now! I want every man down here, gun in hand!"

KIRKPATRICK HIMSELF stood on the steps, with his gun poised while the men in police blue filed past him. Nita twisted her hands. There was no sound in the cellar save for the splashing of the policemen as they moved to close the mouth of that alcove. Nita looked desperately about. She could pull her gun and, perhaps, hold them all captive while Dick made his get-away. She caught the small automatic from her bodice... and a hand clamped rigidly down on her wrist.

"Not this time, Nita," said Kirkpatrick, sternly. "I know he saved your life, but he is a criminal!"

After he had spoken, there was deep silence in the cellar. There was a slow dripping of wine somewhere in the darkness, and that was all. Kirkpatrick lifted his voice.

"All right, Spider," he added quietly. "This time you're trapped. Come out!"

Silence through a long moment, and then the softly mocking laughter of the Spider! *"Come and get me, Kirkpatrick!"*

Kirkpatrick's flashlight, like every other one in that tight cellar, was focused on the entrance to the alcove, and now Kirkpatrick moved steadily sideways. His light moved with him, and he shifted his revolver to be ready.

Nita lifted her face, her eyes closed, and her lips moved silently. It was when she opened her eyes that she started violently. Afterward, she looked down at the wine that lapped around her knees. She began to plead brokenly with Kirkpatrick.

"He's such a brave man, Stanley," she said. "You would never have caught the Iron Man without him. You know that! Let me go! You can't do this to the Spider!"

She threshed her legs in the wine, and the policeman grunted and tightened his hold. Kirkpatrick did not answer. He suddenly made a wide leap sideways, and his light stabbed into the alcove, his gun raked out... She peered into the recess in the wall. There was a man there in a black cape and hat. His hands were stretched high above his head, as if in abject surrender. But Nita's eyes saw that a light length of line held them upward, was looped over the steam pipe.

"So you surrender, Spider!" Kirkpatrick's voice was full of relief. "That was wise of you!"

He moved toward the motionless figure in the recess, and suddenly the light, mocking laughter of the Spider filled all the basement! It seemed to come from everywhere at once, but Nita's keen eyes placed it at once. She saw Wentworth slip from the overhead steam pipe along which he had crawled while the flashlights focused beams beneath him, saw him stand upright on the steps a moment before he laughed.

"Why no, Kirkpatrick," the Spider called gently. "I never surrender. And don't hurt poor Frank Drexler, who was forced to don my robes for a moment. He is quite innocent!"

Finally, Kirkpatrick spotted the source of that voice. He whirled, with his gun raking out, but the light laughter sounded again. There was a flicker of movement at the head of the steps, and then the steel door clanged shut, and a lock snapped into place. Kirkpatrick fired a single shot, and it rang like a gong against the closed door. And laughter still sounded in the cellar from which the Master of Men had escaped.

But it was Nita laughing. "Isn't that too bad, Stanley," she said softly. "I do believe the Spider has 'disappeared' once more!"

THE SPIDER

- ❏ #1: The Spider Strikes — $13.95
- ❏ #2: The Wheel of Death — $13.95
- ❏ #3: Wings of the Black Death — $13.95
- ❏ #4: City of Flaming Shadows — $13.95
- ❏ #5: Empire of Doom! — $13.95
- ❏ #6: Citadel of Hell — $13.95
- ❏ #7: The Serpent of Destruction — $13.95
- ❏ #8: The Mad Horde — $13.95
- ❏ #9: Satan's Death Blast — $13.95
- ❏ #10: The Corpse Cargo — $13.95
- ❏ #11: Prince of the Red Looters — $13.95
- ❏ #12: Reign of the Silver Terror — $13.95
- ❏ #13: Builders of the Dark Empire — $13.95
- ❏ #14: Death's Crimson Juggernaut — $13.95
- ❏ #15: The Red Death Rain — $13.95
- ❏ #16: The City Destroyer — $13.95
- ❏ #17: The Pain Emperor — $13.95
- ❏ #18: The Flame Master — $13.95
- ❏ #19: Slaves of the Crime Master — $13.95
- ❏ #20: Reign of the Death Fiddler — $13.95
- ❏ #21: Hordes of the Red Butcher — $13.95
- ❏ #22: Dragon Lord of the Underworld — $13.95
- ❏ #23: Master of the Death-Madness — $13.95
- ❏ #24: King of the Red Killers — $13.95
- ❏ #25: Overlord of the Damned — $13.95
- ❏ #26: Death Reign of the Vampire King — $13.95
- ❏ #27: Emperor of the Yellow Death — $13.95
- ❏ #28: The Mayor of Hell — $13.95
- ❏ #29: Slaves of the Murder Syndicate — $13.95
- ❏ #30: Green Globes of Death — $13.95
- ❏ #31: The Cholera King — $13.95
- ❏ #32: Slaves of the Dragon — $13.95
- ❏ #33: Legions of Madness — $12.95
- ❏ #34: Laboratory of the Damned — $12.95
- ❏ #35: Satan's Sightless Legion — $12.95
- ❏ #36: The Coming of the Terror — $12.95
- ❏ #37: The Devil's Death-Dwarfs — $12.95
- ❏ #38: City of Dreadful Night — $12.95
- ❏ #39: Reign of the Snake Men — $12.95
- ❏ #40: Dictator of the Damned — $12.95
- ❏ #41: The Mill-Town Massacres — $12.95
- ❏ #42: Satan's Workshop — $12.95
- ❏ #43: Scourge of the Yellow Fangs — $12.95
- ❏ #44: The Devil's Pawnbroker — $12.95
- ❏ #45: Voyage of the Coffin Ship — $12.95
- ❏ #46: The Man Who Ruled in Hell — $13.95
- ❏ #47: Slaves of the Black Monarch — $13.95
- ❏ #48: Machineguns Over the White House — $13.95
- ❏ #49: The City That Dared Not Eat — $13.95
- ❏ #50: Master of the Flaming Horde — $13.95
- ❏ #51: Satan's Switchboard — $13.95
- ❏ #52: Legions of the Accursed Light — $13.95
- ❏ #53: The City of Lost Men — $13.95
- ❏ #54: The Grey Horde Creeps — $13.95
- ❏ #55: City of Whispering Death — $13.95
- ❏ #56: When Thousands Slept in Hell — $13.95
- ❏ #57: Satan's Shakles — $14.95
- ❏ #58: The Emperor From Hell — $14.95
- ❏ #59: The Devil's Candlesticks — $14.95
- ❏ #60: The City That Paid to Die — $14.95
- ❏ #61: The Spider at Bay — $14.95
- ❏ #62: Scourge of the Black Legions — $14.95
- ❏ #63: The Withering Death — $14.95
- ❏ #64: Claws of the Golden Dragon — $14.95
- ❏ #65: The Song of Death — $14.95
- ❏ #66: The Silver Death Reign — $14.95
- ❏ #67: Blight of the Blazing Eye — $14.95
- ❏ #68: King of the Fleshless Legion — $14.95
- ❏ #69: Rule of the Monster Men — $16.95
- ❏ #70: The Spider and the Slaves of Hell — $16.95
- ❏ #71: The Spider and the Fire God — $16.95
- ❏ #72: The Corpse Broker — $16.95
- ❏ #73: The Spider and the Eyeless Legion — $16.95
- ❏ #74: The Spider and the Faceless One — $16.95
- ❏ *NEW:* #75: Satan's Murder Machines — $16.95

THE WESTERN RAIDER

- ❏ #1: Guns of the Damned — $13.95
- ❏ #2: The Hawk Rides Back from Death — $13.95
- ❏ #3: Gun-Call for the Lost Legion — $13.95
- ❏ #4: The Law of Silver Trent — $13.95
- ❏ #5: The Gun-Prayer of Silver Trent — $13.95
- ❏ #6: Silver Trent Rides Alone — $13.95

CAPTAIN SATAN

- ❏ #1: The Mask of the Damned — $13.95
- ❏ #2: Parole for the Dead — $13.95
- ❏ #3: The Dead Man Express — $13.95
- ❏ #4: A Ghost Rides the Dawn — $13.95
- ❏ #5: The Ambassador From Hell — $13.95

DR. YEN SIN

- ❏ #1: Mystery of the Dragon's Shadow — $12.95
- ❏ #2: Mystery of the Golden Skull — $12.95
- ❏ #3: Mystery of the Singing Mummies — $12.95

THE MASKED MARKSMAN

- ❏ #1: Death Takes an Encore — $16.95
- ❏ *NEW:* #2: Death's Understudy — $16.95

ACE G-MAN

- ❏ #1: The Suicide Squad Reports for Death — $14.95
- ❏ #2: Coffins for the Suicide Squad — $14.95

❏ #3: Shells for the Suicide Squad	$14.95
❏ #4: The Suicide Squad in Corpse-Town	$14.95
❏ #5: Wanted–In Three Pine Coffins	$14.95
❏ #6: The Suicide Squad's Dawn Patrol	$14.95
❏ #7: Targets for the Flaming Arrow	$16.95

OPERATOR 5

❏ #1: The Masked Invasion	$13.95
❏ #2: The Invisible Empire	$13.95
❏ #3: The Yellow Scourge	$13.95
❏ #4: The Melting Death	$13.95
❏ #5: Cavern of the Damned	$13.95
❏ #6: Master of Broken Men	$13.95
❏ #7: Invasion of the Dark Legions	$13.95
❏ #8: The Green Death Mists	$13.95
❏ #9: Legions of Starvation	$13.95
❏ #10: The Red Invader	$13.95
❏ #11: The League of War-Monsters	$13.95
❏ #12: The Army of the Dead	$13.95
❏ #13: March of the Flame Marauders	$13.95
❏ #14: Blood Reign of the Dictator	$13.95
❏ #15: Invasion of the Yellow Warlords	$13.95
❏ #16: Legions of the Death Master	$13.95
❏ #17: Hosts of the Flaming Death	$13.95
❏ #18: Invasion of the Crimson Death Cult	$13.95
❏ #19: Attack of the Blizzard Men	$13.95
❏ #20: Scourge of the Invisible Death	$13.95
❏ #21: Raiders of the Red Death	$13.95
❏ #22: War-Dogs of the Green Destroyer	$13.95
❏ #23: Rockets From Hell	$13.95
❏ #24: War-Masters from the Orient	$13.95
❏ #25: Crime's Reign of Terror	$13.95
❏ #26: Death's Ragged Army	$13.95
❏ #27: Patriots' Death Battalion	$13.95
❏ #28: The Bloody Forty-five Days	$13.95
❏ #29: America's Plague Battalions	$13.95
❏ #30: Liberty's Suicide Legions	$13.95
❏ #31: Siege of the Thousand Patriots	$13.95
❏ #32: Patriots' Death March	$14.95
❏ #33: Revolt of the Lost Legions	$14.95
❏ #34: Drums of Destruction	$14.95
❏ #35: The Army Without a Country	$14.95
❏ #36: The Bloody Frontiers	$14.95
❏ #37: The Coming of the Mongol Hordes	$14.95
❏ #38: The Siege That Brought Black Death	$16.95
❏ #39: Revolt of the Devil Men	$16.95
❏ #40: The Suicide Battalion	$16.95
❏ #41: The Day of the Damned	$16.95

RED FINGER

❏ #1: Second-Hand Death	$24.95

G-8 AND HIS BATTLE ACES

❏ #1: The Bat Staffel	$13.95

CAPTAIN COMBAT

❏ #1: The Sky Beast of Berlin	$13.95
❏ #2: Red Wings For the Blood Battalion	$13.95
❏ #3: Low Ceiling For Nazi Hell Hawks	$13.95

DUSTY AYRES AND HIS BATTLE BIRDS

❏ #1: Black Lightning!	$13.95
❏ #2: Crimson Doom	$13.95
❏ #3: The Purple Tornado	$13.95
❏ #4: The Screaming Eye	$13.95
❏ #5: The Green Thunderbolt	$13.95
❏ #6: The Red Destroyer	$13.95
❏ #7: The White Death	$13.95
❏ #8: The Black Avenger	$13.95
❏ #9: The Silver Typhoon	$13.95
❏ #10: The Troposphere F-S	$13.95
❏ #11: The Blue Cyclone	$13.95
❏ #12: The Tesla Raiders	$13.95

MAVERICKS

❏ #1: Five Against the Law	$12.95
❏ #2: Mesquite Manhunters	$12.95
❏ #3: Bait for the Lobo Pack	$12.95
❏ #4: Doc Grimson's Outlaw Posse	$12.95
❏ #5: Charlie Parr's Gunsmoke Cure	$12.95

THE MYSTERIOUS WU FANG

❏ #1: The Case of the Six Coffins	$12.95
❏ #2: The Case of the Scarlet Feather	$12.95
❏ #3: The Case of the Yellow Mask	$12.95
❏ #4: The Case of the Suicide Tomb	$12.95
❏ #5: The Case of the Green Death	$12.95
❏ #6: The Case of the Black Lotus	$12.95
❏ #7: The Case of the Hidden Scourge	$12.95

THE SECRET 6

❏ #1: The Red Shadow	$13.95
❏ #2: House of Walking Corpses	$13.95
❏ #3: The Monster Murders	$13.95
❏ #4: The Golden Alligator	$13.95

CAPTAIN ZERO

❏ #1: City of Deadly Sleep	$13.95
❏ #2: The Mark of Zero!	$13.95
❏ #3: The Golden Murder Syndicate	$13.95